THE

LAW AND CUSTOM OF

PRIMOGENITURE

(BEING AN ESSAY WHICH, JOINTLY WITH ANOTHER, OBTAINED THE YORKE
PRIZE OF THE UNIVERSITY OF CAMBRIDGE).

By PERCEVAL M. LAURENCE, B.A.,
FELLOW OF CORPUS CHRISTI COLLEGE,
WHEWELL SCHOLAR AND MEMBERS' PRIZEMAN IN THE UNIVERSITY OF CAMBRIDGE,
AND OF LINCOLN'S INN,
TANCRED STUDENT IN COMMON LAW.

Le partage des biens, les lois sur ce partage, les successions après la mort de celui qui a eu ce partage ; tout cela ne peut avoir été réglé que par la société, et par conséquent par des lois politiques ou civiles.—Montesquieu, *Esprit des Lois*, xxvi. 6.

CAMBRIDGE:—J. HALL AND SON, TRUMPINGTON STREET.
LONDON:—REEVES AND TURNER, CHANCERY LANE.
1878.

TO

SIR HENRY SUMNER MAINE, K.C.S.I., LL.D., F.R.S., &c., &c.,

MASTER OF TRINITY HALL,

THIS ESSAY IS BY PERMISSION RESPECTFULLY INSCRIBED

IN TOKEN OF THE WRITER'S GRATEFUL SENSE

OF THE INVALUABLE AID HE HAS RECEIVED

IN THE STUDY OF JURISPRUDENCE AND

COMPREHENSION OF HISTORY

FROM THE PUBLICATIONS OF THE AUTHOR OF

"ANCIENT LAW."

PREFACE.

EDMUND YORKE, M.A., late Fellow of St. Catharine's Hall, bequeathed to the University of Cambridge a sum of money for the purpose of founding a Prize for an Essay on the Law of Primogeniture. A scheme for carrying out the bequest received the sanction of the Chancery Division of the High Court in 1875; and it was ordered that a prize should annually be offered for competition for an essay on some subject relating to "the Law of Property, its Principles and History in various Ages and Countries." The prize was first offered in November, 1876, when the subject announced was "The History of the Law of Primogeniture in England, and its effects upon Landed Property." The prize was awarded, in February of this year, to the present essay, together with that sent in by my friend, Mr. C. S. Kenny, LL.M., Fellow and Law Lecturer of Downing College, the two Essays being pronounced by the Examiners to be of equal merit. They are now published, in accordance with the requirements of the University; and it may perhaps be convenient to mention that copies of both essays, bound in a single volume, may be obtained from the publishers.

P. M. L.

LIST OF STATUTES REFERRED TO.

	PAGE.
20 HEN. III. c. 6 (Statute of Merton)	39
3 EDW. I. c. 36 (Westminster the First)	38
13 EDW. I. c. 1 (*De Donis*)	49, 53
18 EDW. I. c. 1 (*Quia emptores*)	45
25 EDW. I. c. 5, 6 (*Confirmatio Chartarum*)	38
1 EDW. III. c. 12 (Tenants *in capite*)	45, 53
34 EDW. III. c. 13 (Fines)	58
9 RIC. II. c. 3 (Life Tenants)	57, 60
15 RIC. II. c. 5 (Mortmain)	55
1 RIC. III. c. 7 (Fines)	58
4 HEN. VII. c. 24 (Proclamation of fines)	58
32 HEN. VIII. c. 1 (Wills)	45, 59
33 HEN. VIII. c. 39 (Crown Debts)	56
34 & 35 HEN. VIII. c. 5 (Wills)	45
12 CAR. II. c. 24 (Feudal tenures)	59
22 & 23 CAR. II. c. 10 (Distribution)	135
1 JAC. II. c. 17 (Ibid)	135
1 JAC. VII. c. 22 (Scotland—Tallies)	64
4 & 5 ANNE c. 16 (Attornment)	39
3 & 4 WILL. IV. c. 74 (Fines and Recoveries)	59, 62
3 & 4 WILL. IV. c. 106 (Descents)	43
10 GEO. III. c. 51 (Scotch entails)	66
8 & 9 VICT. c. 106 (Contingent remainders)	62
11 & 12 VICT. c. 36 (Scotch entails)	67
15 & 16 VICT. c. 51 (Copyholds)	106
16 & 17 VICT. c. 94 (Scotch entails)	67
17 & 18 VICT. c. 113 (Mortgage debts)	56
19 & 20 VICT. c. 120 (Leases and Sales)	106
21 & 22 VICT. c. 94 (Copyholds)	106
25 & 26 VICT. c. 53 (Title)	111
30 & 31 VICT. c. 69 (Mortgage debts)	56
33 & 34 VICT. c. 23 (Attainders)	65
37 & 38 VICT. c. 78 (Vendor and Purchaser)	110
38 & 39 VICT. c. 87 (Land transfer)	110
38 & 39 VICT. c. 92 (Agricultural holdings)	107
39 & 40 VICT. c. 74 (Ditto amendment)	107
40 & 41 VICT. c. 18 (Settled Estates)	107

TABLE OF CONTENTS.

SECTION VI.—THE LAW OF INTESTATE SUCCESSION 133
SECTION VII.—ON THE POLICY OF CHANGE IN THE LAND LAWS ... 150
INDEX 157

THE

Law and Custom of Primogeniture.

SECTION I.—THE ORIGIN OF PRIMOGENITURE IN THE EARLY HISTORY OF ARYAN INSTITUTIONS.

THE history of the custom of Primogeniture in England cannot be satisfactorily treated without some preliminary examination of the circumstances, conditions, and laws—whether imposed by sovereign power or sanctioned by custom and tradition—in a word, of the social atmosphere in which the privileges of the eldest son first arose. And this takes us back to a very remote period in the history of society. It is true that the traces of any similar institution which we are able to discover in the recorded history of those ancient peoples with whose annals we are most familiar are extremely slight; and to a superficial observer they would perhaps appear most palpably to disclose themselves in the records of a branch of the human family unconnected with our own—those Semitic tribes, I mean, into whose social institutions we obtain some precarious* insight from the incidental testimony of Scriptural history, and from whom it is improbable that any material portion of Aryan law or custom has been borrowed or derived. At the same time, the very scantiness of these vestiges in one sense increases the importance of their careful examination. For though we are unable to affirm the existence of what we understand by

* By this epithet I of course merely mean that the Old Testament neither contains, nor affects to contain, a philosophical account of the ancient Jewish institutions. It is in the main a political history of the vicissitudes of a theocratic State.

Primogeniture among the ancient Greeks and Romans of the South, or the Franks and Gauls of Northern and Western Europe, we may yet feel some confidence that a patient scrutiny will reveal its germs. Otherwise it is not easy to comprehend how the period of anarchy which gave birth to Feudalism should have also produced this institution as its inseparable appendage. The seeds must have been lurking somewhere; and it is interesting to observe the conditions which brought the embryo into light. "There are always certain ideas," writes Sir Henry Maine, "existing antecedently on which the sense of convenience works, and of which it can do no more than form some new combination; and to find these ideas in the present case is exactly the problem."*

In the chapter wherein the above passage occurs, Sir Henry makes it probable, for reasons which I shall subsequently endeavour to develop, that the origin of this custom is to be found in the primitive family life which confronts us on the very threshold of Aryan society. It may at least be affirmed with safety that we need not pursue our backward search to an earlier period than that in which the family ties and the family relations, knit together by the paternal power, are supreme, while society itself is based on consanguinity alone. It is not here asserted that this is the most archaic form of social organisation which modern inquiry is able to detect. It is possible that there may have been a præ-Aryan period, of which all that we know as Aryan—that social life of which the above are the most salient characteristics—was merely a development, instead of being, as until recently was assumed, the immemorial heritage of one alone among the great races of mankind. It is possible that as the family, according to the testimony of Aristotle and of experience, produced the tribe, so in a yet more primitive period the family itself arose out of a modification of an antecedent tribal system. There can be little hesitation in attributing this modification to the introduction of monogamy. Mr. McLennan and other writers

* Ancient Law, p. 233.

have shewn that there is some reason to believe that monogamy was generally preceded by a præ-historic era in which polyandry was the ordinary form of sexual union. In barbarous ages, as among many savage tribes of the present day, the practice of female infanticide produced a vast disproportion between the male and the female population. The feminine sex was regarded as an unproductive luxury, of which the preservation could only be tolerated under severe restrictions. If a tribe were weak, policy forbade it to burden itself with a superfluous number of beings whom nature had incapacitated for performing substantial service in the battle or the chase. When it became stronger, it seemed both convenient and agreeable to obtain such women as were required by conquest, violence or theft. Tribes once endogamous by necessity thus became exogamous by choice; and an opportunity sometimes occurred under these circumstances, when warlike success had produced riches, for the chiefs of a powerful tribe to go to the other extreme, and substitute polygyny—or polygamy in the ordinary sense—for the converse practice of polyandry.* It is by this latter custom alone, repulsive as it may seem to modern feeling, that we are able to explain the rule which we know to have prevailed, by which relationships were traced exclusively through the female parent. Another stage was reached when, as the security and stability of life increased, perhaps simultaneously with the introduction of agriculture, a return to endogamy once more took place. Mr. McLennan indeed shews, as might have been expected, that this order of events was not invariable; but their course was probably in the large majority of instances somewhat as indicated above. The era—usually polyandrous—of "capture" gave place to a—frequently polygynous—era of "purchase," which was itself eventually superseded by a era of "presents," in the main coincident with the establishment of monogamy, and the beginning of Aryan civilisation. Without here asserting any absolute generic difference between

---

* Traces of polyandry are to be found in some of the institutions which we know to have existed at Sparta.

"Aryan" and other races, we are at least justified in saying that we meet with no Aryan people, in which what is best known as the "patriarchal system" did not in some form or other exist. At the same time it would probably be incorrect to reverse the proposition, and affirm that every race so organised, at the earliest period at which history begins, was of Aryan origin; since we have abundant evidence that a similar state of society—though always complicated and debased by the practice of polygamy—prevailed among several of the Semitic tribes.

The extension of our social retrospect to so early a period in the history of institutions as that which coincides with the establishment of monogamy, may perhaps suggest a reproach analogous to that incurred by the historian of the Trojan war, who commenced his narrative with an account of the incubation of Leda's egg. However, as has already been remarked, in the more advanced stages of Aryan society we meet with but scanty evidence of any *proprietary* privileges attached to the position of eldest son. Such privileges may possibly have once existed; but when the family had grown into the village community, still more when it had been absorbed in the organisation of the city, they had almost entirely disappeared. We find little trace of any similar institution among the Hindus, the Greeks or Romans, the ancient Germans or the ancient Kelts. And yet a brief examination of the main features of the succession laws which prevailed among these nations will not, I believe, be altogether irrelevant to our present purpose.

It is well known that in India the partition of the family inheritance has never been an ordinary result of the demise of its head. It was, in fact, this very retention of domicile and land in common which must have originally produced those village communities with the nature of which the observers of Indian institutions have made us so familiar.[*] It appears, however, that so far from the eldest son having any rights of ownership superior to those enjoyed by his

---

[*] See, for example, "Tagore Law Lectures, 1874-75: The Law relating to the Land Tenures of Lower Bengal." By Arthur Phillips, M.A., Officiating Standing Counsel to the Government of India. P. 10, "The Origin of the Village."

brothers, the native customary law vested in every son, from the moment of his birth, a share in the paternal estate, and indeed gave him a technical right, seldom actually exercised, of demanding, on attaining full age, a partition of the property. The consent of every male child was always necessary to its alienation, and whenever a division was effected, each received an equal portion.* This practice in its main features still subsists. Indian law is as solicitous as that of England in its efforts to preserve the connection between each family and its ancestral lands, but its *modus operandi*, as thus appears, is widely different. The *representative* rights of the eldest son must be subsequently considered; but it may safely be asserted that it is not until a comparatively recent period in the history of the Indian law that any traces disclose themselves of proprietary advantage being involved in priority of birth. We for the first time encounter something analogous to our own system of Primogeniture when we arrive at the period of the Zemindars and Talookdars, classes which owe their importance to the Muhammadan period, and whose proper position with reference to the land and the rival claims of the village communities has for many years presented so perplexing a problem to the British Government.† Mr. Arthur Phillips, in his valuable and exhaustive lectures on the land law of Lower Bengal, inclines to the belief that the Zemindars were in many cases the lineal descendants of the village Headmen.‡ The Zemindars, however, gradually absorbed the rights and functions of many such local heads, and for the purpose of collecting the revenue represented to the Muhammadan, and subsequently to the British Government, not a single village but an entire district, or fiscal division. It appears from Dr. Hunter's admirable work on Orissa

---

* See Maine, *Ancient Law*, pp. 228, 233, 280. The sons as a rule were only *recommended* by the Law of Manu and regular custom to provide their sisters with portions. See *La Cité Antique*, par M. Fustel de Coulanges, p. 81.

† See Maine, *Village Communities*, pp. 149-161. With regard to the *origin* of this class, see especially p. 156.

‡ Tagore Law Lectures, *ut supra*, pp. 31, 64, 65.

that, as the result of careful investigation and personal observation in that province, he arrived at conclusions with regard to the origin and nature of this class of superior landholders not greatly dissimilar to those which Mr. Phillips deduces from his researches in Bengal.* We are especially indebted to Dr. Hunter for a lucid explanation of the manner in which, under the lax rule of the Musalmans, the Zemindars and Talookdars grew from mere revenue officers and local representatives into the position of proprietors, claiming, though without complete success, an indefeasible right to the soil. I now come to the point which has induced me to dwell on the position of these Zemindars. Their power arose in turbulent times, when the central Government was extremely weak, little able to resist the encroachments of strong local chieftains, and scarcely anxious to do so, provided the customary revenue dues were punctually paid to the imperial treasury. The Zemindars and other subordinate landholders owed their position to a gradual and fraudulent assumption, and could not reckon on retaining it except by their own strength. We hear of their unjustifiable pretensions as early as the beginning of the fourteenth century, in the reign of Ala-ood-deen. Now in this era of violence and —to borrow a convenient phrase of Sir Fitzjames Stephen— of "dormant anarchy," it became of the utmost importance to the Zemindars to convert the system of *appointments* to the posts they held into a system of *hereditary succession*. The feeble government of the Muhammadans was unable to assert its rights, and the customary mandate of appointment, on the demise of a Zemindar, dwindled into a tacit recognition of his son and successor.† It is very interesting to observe that it was under these circumstances and among this class that a system of Primogeniture seems to have first arisen in India. The encroaching landholders appear to have discovered that the only method of securing the privileges they had won lay in transmitting their pos-

---

* Orissa. By W. W. Hunter, LL.D. London: Smith, Elder, and Co. 1872. See Vol. II., pp. 214-230, 239, 240, 255-261.

† Ibid, p. 227.

sessions to the eldest son alone. Mr. Phillips, indeed, considers that this method of succession, which is almost confined to the superior Zemindaries, points to a descent of the Zemindars from the ancient Rajahs, the *raj*—which was of course in the main a *political* office—having undoubtedly descended in this manner.* It is somewhat remarkable that this Indian form of Primogeniture was on the whole unfavourably regarded by the British administrators up to the time of the Permanent Settlements effected by Lord Cornwallis in Lower Bengal in 1793, and subsequently, in 1815, in the province of Orissa. The eleventh Regulation of 1793 deals with this matter; and after reciting that "by custom originating in considerations of financial convenience," some of the most extensive Zemindaries descended by Primogeniture; that such a custom was repugnant both to Hindu and Muhammadan laws, and subversive of the rights of the other members of the family; that it moreover hindered improvements, "from the proprietors of those large estates not having the means, or being unable to bestow the attention requisite for bringing into cultivation the extensive tracts of waste land comprised in them;"† it was accordingly enacted that for the future, on any Zemindar or independent Talookdar dying intestate, his property was to be equally divided among his lineal representatives.‡ The equal division of landed property on intestacy is earnestly advocated by a section of law reformers and economists in England; the discussion of the policy of such a change must be reserved for another section; it is, however, worth while to notice that it was considered desirable to establish a uniform rule to that effect in India more than eighty years ago. At the same time it should be added that in the year 1800 a subsequent regulation excluded from the operation of the law of 1793 certain districts in which Primogeniture prevailed as a general local custom, and not merely as the

* Tagore Law Lectures, *ut supra*, pp. 64, 99.
† This view of the effect of large holdings on the cultivation of waste lands in India differs very widely from that put forward by Sir Henry Maine: see *Village Communities*, pp. 161-165.
‡ Tagore Law Lectures, p. 390.

usage of particular estates. "To this day," says Sir George Campbell, "I believe that it is not very clear what estates do, and what do not, descend to a single heir; but the matter is not so important because the courts have recognised the power of Hindus to make wills. *The Hindu laws say nothing of wills*, and it is very doubtful whether they should have been admitted; but the courts acting on English precedents* having once admitted them, this curious result has followed that, in the absence of any provisions to limit them, the power of a Hindu in Bengal to tie up his property by will is almost unlimited."†

Were it not for the extreme importance to the history of social development of Indian institutions, such as we either see them now, or know them to have formerly existed, and

---

* Some very interesting remarks on the effect of English law and English precedents on the Indian Courts, Sudder as well as Supreme, are to be found in Maine's *Village Communities*, pp. 36-47. The following passage may be quoted as illustrating Sir George Campbell's observations:—"The judges who presided over the most important of these courts very early recognised the existence of testamentary power among the Hindus. It seems that, in the province of Lower Bengal, where the village system had been greatly broken up, the head of the household had the power of disposing of his patrimony during his life. Whether he could dispose of it at death, and thus execute a disposition in any way resembling a will, has always been a much disputed question, which, however, contemporary opinion rather inclines towards answering in the negative. However that may be, the power of making a will was soon firmly established among the Hindus of Lower Bengal by, or through the influence of, the English lawyers who first entered the country."—p. 40. He then proceeds to give some examples of the capricious manner in which this power has occasionally been exercised. In one case, decided after the publication of *Village Communities*, "a Brahmin of high lineage, who made a fortune at the Calcutta Bar, aimed at disinheriting or excluding from the main line of succession a son who had embraced Christianity." Writing *pendente lite* Sir Henry adds:— "All I can say without impropriety is that, in those parts of India in which the collective holding of property has not decayed as much as it has done in Lower Bengal, the liberty of testation claimed would clearly be foreign to the indigenous system of the country. That system is one of common enjoyment by village communities, and, inside those communities, by families. The individual has almost no power of disposing of his property; even if he be chief of his household, the utmost he can do, as a rule, is to regulate the disposition of his property among his children within certain very narrow limits." Pp. 41-42. The validity of the will here referred to was subsequently affirmed by the Privy Council (Ganendro Mohun Tagore *v.* Rajah Jotendro Mohun Tagore and others, Law Reports, Indian Appeals, 1874, p. 387).

† Systems of Land Tenure in Various Countries, p. 177.

the remarkable analogy which a careful scrutiny has so often detected between portions of the Indian land-law and that which prevails, or, up to comparatively modern times, has prevailed in Western Europe, I should fear that too much space had been already occupied with the discussion of topics only indirectly connected with the immediate subject of this essay. The law of intestate succession in Greece and at Rome has been so often and so fully discussed that it may be here passed over with the briefest mention. At Athens, as is well known, the sons in such case inherited in equal shares, being, however, under an obligation to maintain their sisters and provide them with marriage portions. Where there were no sons, the daughters were still excluded from succession, the property going, subject to a similar condition, to the nearest male kinsman. At Sparta, the women occupied a better position; and we learn that at the period when Aristotle wrote his *Politics* the number of heiresses was very considerable, so great, indeed, as to have been regarded by the philosopher as presenting a grave political danger. We know that at Rome the inheritance by women of the property of an intestate father, who had been enrolled on the census, was circumscribed by the Voconian Law; and we know also that by the legislation of Justinian daughters were placed on the same footing in respect to succession to property on intestacy as sons. The period, however, during which the Lex Voconia exercised a sensible influence—before its evasion by the system of *fidei-commissa*—has not been ascertained with precision; and there is still greater uncertainty as to the rules of distribution which prevailed in the early Republican period. Some controversy has arisen as to the exact interpretation of the well-known fragment of the twelve tables, "*Si intestato moritur cui suus hæres nec sit, adgnatus proximus familiam habeto.*"[*] The general opinion, adopted among others by Hugo, Ortolan and Maine, is that, where an intestate father left surviving children, the paternal inheritance was equally divided

[*] See Ortolan, Histoire de la Législation Romaine, Third Edition, p. 90, nt. 1.

among all the unemancipated sons and daughters. M. Fustel de Coulanges, on the other hand, argues with considerable plausibility in favour of the opposite view, and maintains that daughters were excluded at Rome as well as in India and at Athens;[*] and in any case it cannot be doubted that a merely nominal equality on their part must have been of little efficacity, on account of the system of perpetual tutelage to which we know them to have been subjected. With regard to the sons, however, the fact that they succeeded to the paternal estate in equal shares has seldom been contested. Mr. McCulloch, it is true, has endeavoured to raise some doubts on the point. "It is not easy to suppose," he says, "that the equal division of property among the sons would be generally practised by parties who resorted to such means (he refers to the custom of adoption) for perpetuating its descent in the same lines." This presumption, however, would appear to rest on a very doubtful and probably deceptive analogy; and it certainly does not seem an irresistible inference from the circumstance that in one particular the Roman method of perpetuating family estates differed—because actuated, as we know, by widely different motives—very greatly from our own, that therefore in another particular it must have resembled that with which we are ourselves familiar. Mr. McCulloch proceeds to adduce the existence of the well-known *latifundia* in the later Republican and Imperial periods, and their devolution in regular lines, as a proof that the Roman paterfamilias was accustomed to devise his property in a method more nearly resembling that of Primogeniture than that of equal division.[†] When, however, we take into consideration the fact that such hereditary estates were probably the reverse of numerous, and that our information concerning their character and origin is extremely scanty, and when we also remember the many opportunities which a Roman nobleman of the period referred to, especially if engaged in the work of provincial government, must have

[*] La Cité Antique, Livre ii., c. 7. Le Droit de Succession, pp. 81, 82. See also, A Treatise on the Succession to Property Vacant by Death, by Mr. McCulloch, pp. 18—21.

[†] A Treatise, &c., *ut supra*, p. 20, note.

commanded for enriching himself, we shall certainly hesitate to draw so bold a conclusion from such slight and precarious premises. It is more probable that the Roman testament was frequently employed in order to restore to the eldest son a share in the family property, which, owing to his emancipation from the paternal power, he would have failed to receive on a distribution *ab intestato* than that he habitually acquired by his father's bequest any extensive proprietary advantages over the younger children.

Enough has been said to shew that among the Hindus, Greeks and Romans, intestate succession was seldom if ever regulated by the principle of Primogeniture. Neither was it frequently adopted in the testamentary dispositions by which the course of the law was modified and controlled. It is important, moreover, to observe that the restrictions which limited the disposition by will of landed property in early times were always very great. In the Hindu law, as has already been pointed out, there was no such thing as a true will. At Athens there was none until the time of Solon; and that which was then legalised—but only in the event of a testator having no surviving children—was so partial in its operation as to be accurately described as a merely "inchoate" testament. A striking passage in the *Laws* of Plato attests the prejudice experienced by the ancient promulgators of codes against any claim to a posthumous control over landed property.* Among the Germans, as among the Hindus, the allodial estate descended in equal shares—though not habitually divided—to all the

---

* Plato's view is, that each man belongs not to himself, but to his family and city; moreover, he distrusts an old man's judgment, perverted, it may be, by declining faculties, and the interested flattery of those around him. The main anxiety of the philosopher is to preserve the ancestral lots—5040 in number—intact; for this purpose it is desirable to restrict the number of children to two, to represent their parents in the succeeding generation. The hereditary property must descend entire to *one* son; but if the father has more than one, he may determine by will on whom it is to devolve. Whatever other property the father may possess—his personal acquisitions, in fact—he may distribute *among his children* in any proportion he pleases.—Plato, Legg. xi., pp. 923, 924; Grote, Plato, Vol. III., pp. 434-436. The latter remarks on the general coincidence of tone between the philosopher and the prevalent Attic sentiment on these points.

sons, on the parent's death.* We know that the rules which regulated the Irish system of Gavelkind were equally rigid. It is true that Sir Henry Maine considers it probable that, as the Irish Gavelkind was only an archaic form of the familiar custom still prevalent in the county of Kent and certain other districts in England, so the Irish Tanistry was really the form of succession from which the English Primogeniture itself descended;† but it is important to notice that Tanistry, like many other of the ancient privileges of the eldest son to which I shall shortly draw attention, was rather a *political* than a *proprietary* institution; it determined the right to the signory or chieftainship of the tribe or sept, and any lands which the Tanaist acquired therewith were incidental and not essential to his prerogative. In the early history of feudalism in England we find similar restrictions—of the gradual relaxation of which a full account must be reserved for a succeeding section—on testamentary alienation of the demesne land; and it is not unreasonable to conjecture that they were to some extent formed on the model of those rules which, prior to the introduction of feudalism, determined the succession to the allodial domain. As early as the reign of Henry I., the distinction between inherited property and that acquired by the independent exertions of the owner— a distinction which may be said to have formed in almost all Aryan societies a landmark in the history of the right of alienation—was expressly recognised by the common law. *Acquisitiones suas,* says the compilation known as the Seventieth Law of that monarch, *det cui magis velit: si Bocland‡ autem habeat quam ei parentes sui dederint, non mittat eam extra cognationem suam.*

* Heredes tamen successoresque sui cuique liberi, *et nullum testamentum.* Si liberi non sunt, proximus gradus in possessione fratres, patrui, avunculi.— Tac. Germ. 20. See also Maine, Ancient Law, p. 228 ; and Early History of Institutions, p. 199.

† Early History of Institutions, p. 186.

‡ *Bocland* or "book-land" was that granted to individuals, in the period previous to the Norman invasion, by *charter.* It was contrasted with the *folcland,* or land of the people, which seems to have greatly resembled the Roman *ager publicus*: it could be *occupied* by individuals as tenants of the State, but the king could not make grants out of it without the consent of the Witan.

The result of the foregoing summary would appear to be that the early institutions of India and Greece, of Germany, Ireland and England, recognised the principle of equal distribution on intestacy, sometimes among all the children, sometimes among the sons alone, occasionally, as in Ireland, among a class of kinsmen who formed the sept, and who appear to have practically corresponded to the Roman agnates; wills were either unknown, or strictly confined in their operation to acquisitions, or movables, or "personal property." At Rome, it is true, the case at first sight appears to have been somewhat different. We know that at the very early period when practically every citizen was a member of a *gens*, wills could only be made publicly in the Comitia Curiata, and with the express consent of the testator's Gentiles. But by the time of the decemviral legislation these restrictions had evidently become extremely burdensome, and we accordingly find in the Fifth Table the famous clause, *Uti legassit super pecunia tutelave suæ rei ita ius esto*. Sir Henry Maine thinks there can be no doubt that this formula was intended to sanction the plebeian or nuncupative testament by mancipation; but very different views have been maintained by other eminent authorities; and its precise significance is still to some extent a matter of doubt. What I wish, however, in this place to particularly point out is that this fragment is probably itself *fragmentary*; and that it is extremely dangerous to construe it, in ignorance of its immediate context, as if it necessarily involved a plenary power of disinheriting the *suus hæres*, or natural heir. That such a power was at a later period occasionally exercised, and that legislation was found necessary to check its abuse, is sufficiently well known;[*] but there seems no reason to assume with Sir Henry Maine that it was actually conceded by the decemvirs, in the confident expectation that it would never be exercised. The law of Solon contains the words διάθεσθαι ὅπως ἄν ἐθέλῃ; had it not been that a limiting condition—ἄν μὴ παῖδες ὦσι—immediately precedes them, we

---

[*] See especially Ancient Law, pp. 215-217.

should have imagined that it also conferred an unlimited liberty of bequest. It is surely by no means impossible that the Roman statute proceeded to add, or had previously contained, some such clause as *si cui nulli sint liberi*. In this case the rights of the children would be carefully preserved; and if the permission applied only to the plebeians, there were at that time no Gentiles, possibly in the technical sense no Agnates, whose rights could be infringed.*

It appears to be worth while to briefly consider the reasons which in early times produced this strict connection between the family and the land, and which so constantly relegated the actual possessor to a position little superior to that of a life tenant. It is indeed only from an examination of this point that we are able to comprehend the important privileges which, notwithstanding all that has been said, undoubtedly attached to the position of eldest son. Our explanation of this question must necessarily depend on the solution which we prefer to accept of another and far wider problem, to which only the slightest and most cursory allusion can here be made. What was the tie which bound the ancient family together? Why did society at a primitive period assume the shape and organisation which we know that it presented? Two conflicting answers to this question have been suggested, both of which appear to contain a certain amount of truth; while at the same time each hypothesis has, I think, been unduly pushed to account for phenomena which may be best explained by the rival theory. According to the view of which Sir Henry Maine—a writer to whose works, in any investigation belonging to this department of inquiry, it is almost impossible to avoid the most frequent reference—is the principal exponent, the reply to the question suggested above is extremely simple. Society was entirely based on consanguinity because in its earlier stages there was no other bond by which it could possibly be held together. The rules by which authority was maintained, property administered, and

* By the mature jurisprudence of the Empire we know that the legitimate claims of the children were jealously protected; the *legitima portio* was fixed by the Code of Justinian as one-half or one-third of the patrimony, according as the children did or did not exceed four in number.

its devolution regulated, in the Joint Undivided Family, the Village Community, the Sept, the Tribe, and the archaic State, existed because they were emphatically natural, and because it could not possibly have occurred to those who framed and obeyed them to frame or obey laws of any other kind. This view is of course substantially the same as that adopted by Aristotle, in the opening chapters of the *Politics*, where he explains that before kings and lawgivers arose each family was under the absolute government of its own head—who exercised an authority theoretically as complete as that of Homer's Cyclops—and that it was out of these isolated groups that the κώμη and ultimately the πόλις grew.

We are, however, at present more immediately concerned with the counter-theory, of which the most complete exposition has been given in M. Fustel de Coulanges' interesting monograph on *La Cité Antique*, and which has been warmly adopted by the latest English historian of Greece, Sir George Cox. According to M. de Coulanges, the ancient family was knit together exclusively by the influence of a religious feeling, or, as we should say, of a superstition of the grossest kind. He thus explains the tenacity with which it resisted all modifications from without, and its comparative inaccessibility to the solvent influence of civic life. Similarly, Sir George Cox regards the Family as an extremely unmalleable institution, against which the State, strengthened in the contest by extraneous elements, had to contend as best it could, and is thus led to re-echo the bitter complaint of the Epicurean poet against all the evils which religion was able to counsel and suggest.* The superstition referred to consisted in a belief that the dead ancestor of the family still lived within the tomb, that his comfort and well-being depended on the assiduity with which his material wants were gratified by his descendants, and that he was able and inclined, if neglected or despised, to exercise a malign influence on the future prosperity of his house. There can be no doubt of the extreme ingenuity of this hypothesis; it accounts for much in ancient society which had hitherto

* Cox's History of Greece, Vol. I., chap. ii., pp. 10-26.

baffled explanation; and there is no lack of evidence to believe that the superstitious belief in the duty of propitiating an eponymous progenitor did exercise a very extensive influence on the thoughts and actions of our Aryan ancestors.* At the same time it is almost equally certain that M. de Coulanges has carried his theory much too far, and that it in many points requires to be supplemented and corrected by the simpler view of Aristotle and Maine. The influence of religious feeling is too often pressed to account for phenomena of which other and more obvious explanations may without difficulty be found. Moreover—to adopt the phrase used by Austin, in his celebrated analysis of the theory of an Original Covenant—the explanation of M. de Coulanges is in more than one particular "not only superfluous but inefficient." It is thrust in where it is not wanted, to account for circumstances for which it could not in itself afford a sufficient reason. Let us take for instance the ancient prohibition of celibacy. We know that voluntary celibacy among some nations, as in Sparta, involved civil degradation; and that in almost every ancient state it was severely reprobated by public opinion.† M. de Coulanges accounts for this by the necessity of maintaining the *cultus* of the departed, of providing the dead ancestor with *le repas funèbre*, and of maintaining a perpetual fire on the paternal hearth.‡ It is obvious, however, that such a requirement would not in a large family create a general obligation; if the eldest son married, and had a family, all these objects would be duly fulfilled, even should all his brothers remain single. And yet there is not the slightest reason to suppose

* It is worth while to compare with the first and second books of *La cité Antique*, pp. 1-134, and the chapter of Cox's history cited immediately above, Sir H. Maine's observations on the paramount importance attached by the Hindu law of succession to the due performance of the funeral obsequies.—*Ancient Law*, pp. 193, 194.

† Cf. Plutarch, Lycurgus: Apophth. Laced. Pollux, III., 48. Dion. Hal., IX., 22. ὁ γὰρ ἀρχαῖος αὐτῶν νόμος γαμεῖν τ' ἠνάγκαζε τοὺς ἐν ἡλικίᾳ καὶ τὰ γεννώμενα ἅπαντα ἐπάναγκες τρέφειν. He is speaking of the alleged nearly complete extirpation of the Fabian Gens, at the Cremera, B.C. 475. Similarly Cicero, *De Legibus*, III., 3. 7, Censores. . . . caelibes esse prohibento.

‡ Book II., c. 3, p. 51.

that marriage was more incumbent where there was only one representative of the family than where there were several, or on the eldest in a greater degree than on the youngest son. There can be little doubt that in early times celibacy was penalised—just as at a later period, when morals had become more corrupt, marriage was encouraged by enactments like the *ius trium liberorum*—solely or mainly for reasons of State policy, and because it was considered advisable to maintain and increase for military and social purposes the number of legitimate citizens in each State. Other instances might readily be found of deductions from this theory equally plausible, and equally devoid of substantial warrant.

At the same time, what may be called the "religious" theory undoubtedly constitutes one of the many valuable contributions to our knowledge of the early history of institutions, for which we have in recent years been indebted to the patient application of the comparative method of inquiry. It has been exaggerated and, in the hands of some of its less careful exponents, almost caricatured; yet it assuredly contains very much which is demonstrably true, and of extreme importance. The earliest form of religious rites evidently took the shape of a worship of the dead, which their lineal descendants were bound to scrupulously maintain, and which could not be offered without gross impiety by any but the scions of the house. Hence, if not entirely, at least in great measure arose the importance universally attached to the preservation of the continuity of the family, the violent prejudice entertained against the alienation of its hereditary land, and the heavy penalties with which Hindoo, Greek, and Roman law agreed in visiting the removal of ancient boundaries. Hence, too, may be best explained the absence, in the earliest time, of all conception of testamentary power, and the manner in which, when the increasing value and quantity of other kinds of property had engendered a liberty of bequest, permission to dispose by will of the paternal estate was, as has been shewn above, at first so rigorously refused. Hence, too, and hence alone, we can understand the real meaning of those *sacra* which still form a material part of the succession to a Hindu's estate, and which at Rome in time became so burdensome that the juris-consult of the age of Cicero found no more fertile field for his ingenuity than in devising methods of conveyance which should separate them from the soil and elude their obligation. Many years before, a parasite in one of the comedies of Plautus had found the strongest expression of the value which he set on a patron's hospitality, by exclaiming that "at present prices, a dinner is as good as an inheritance unencumbered by the *sacra*,"* and the point of the joke doubtless did not fail to be appreciated by every citizen who owned a plot of land.

The following considerations will, I think, justify the apparent digression concerning the nature of the ancient family on which I have ventured. When it is clearly seen that the continuity of the family and the maintenance of its ancestral rites practically formed the basis of archaic society, on which the whole superstructure was gradually raised, it will become equally evident that this continuity, all important as it was, could not possibly have been maintained for any length of time without a species of Primogeniture. We have now, in fact, arrived at that germ of the modern institution which I began by predicting that a careful examination of the opinions and social organisation of our ancestors would infallibly reveal. As long as the family was an independent institution, and so long, after the State had grown up around it, as it maintained its distinctive character of an *imperium in imperio*, it must have always had a single head, who was at once its lawgiver and its priest. He was also the sole administrator of the ancestral land. His position, of course, was far removed from that of a genuine owner; it was rather that of a trustee, and the *cestui que trust*, if we follow the view of M. de Coulanges, was the eponymous progenitor, together with the descendants yet to come. His character, in fact, was essentially representative; and he doubtless knew no indulgences and opportunities for enjoyment denied to the other members of

---

* Cena hac annonast sine sacris hereditas.—Trinum. 2, 4, 83.

the household. He administered a common fund for the equal benefit of all. To strangers he alone was responsible for the misdeeds of his kinsfolk; and he had an exclusive right to the emoluments they acquired. On the death of such an one, who filled his place? It obviously was unsusceptible of joint occupancy, and must, we can scarcely doubt, have devolved on the eldest son. In India, it was the eldest son who performed the funeral obsequies of his sire, and according to the law prevalent in some districts he received, in the rare event of division, a double portion of the patrimony, probably in consideration of this solemn office. In Greece, we know that each house and each clan had its peculiar rites, which they met on appointed days to celebrate, and which manifestly presupposed the perpetual existence of an individual representative of every family. It is scarcely possible to imagine that the case was different at Rome. We learn that in later days, when the paternal domain was occasionally divided, the *sacra* were apportioned also; we may hence conclude that up to a more or less advanced period in Roman history they had been usually transmitted intact. Moreover, when we consider how small the value of such hereditary land must ordinarily have been in proportion to the gains which a Roman patrician was able to derive from conquest in Italy or abroad, or from the exercise of professional pursuits, it does not seem unreasonable to suggest that in many cases the younger brothers preferred to leave their father's land as well as his house in the hands of the eldest son, rather than be burdened with their share of the religious expenses it entailed. Such arrangements were probably far from rare. The younger son in Greece or Rome must have often migrated to a colony, or been adopted by a childless parent, or married the only child of another landholder, or received the share of land belonging to an extinct family, or made his fortune in the forum or the field. Although the fact that equal succession was in both these countries the principle of the law may be regarded as incontestable, it by no means follows that the younger children always claimed their share in a "universal succession" which must frequently have been embarrassing, and sometimes, as long as there was no *beneficium inventarii*, the source of positive pecuniary loss. The most ancient feeling on the subject of heritage seems to be indicated by one of the older texts in the Laws of Manu, which De Coulanges translates as follows: "L'âiné prend possession du patrimoine entier, et les autres frères vivent sous son autorité comme s'ils vivaient sous celle de leur père. Le fils aîné acquitte la dette envers les ancêtres; il doit donc tout avoir."* If we bear in mind the foregoing explanation of the real character of the possession thus enjoyed by the eldest brother, we shall have no difficulty in reconciling this precept with the theoretical equality of all. The laws which authorise a partition of the inheritance are said to be of later date. Turning once more to Athenian law, we find an incidental confirmation of the suggestion hazarded above— that the paternal "demesne" was usually retained by the eldest son—in an oration of Demosthenes. In the speech on behalf of Phormio, it is stated that Apollodorus had inherited his father's house by the privilege of the eldest son; "he got the lodging-house under the will by right of Primogeniture," as Mr. Kennedy translates the passage.† From the speech against Bœotus *de nomine*, we further learn that the eldest son alone preserved the family patronymic. A careful examination of the authorities on Attic law would very probably supply evidence of other similar privileges. The really important point lies in the circumstance that while any proprietary advantages which may have once existed have almost entirely disappeared from view under the influence of ancient civilisation, the political or representative importance of the eldest son seems to have diminished with far less rapidity. In India, up to the present day, when the affairs of a village community are entrusted to the management of a single head, he is usually, in theory at least, the eldest son of the eldest line. Such was also very

* Laws of Manu, ix. 105-107, 126. *Cité Antique*, p. 92.

† πρεσβεῖα λαβὼν τὴν συνοικίαν κατὰ τὴν διαθήκην ἔχει. Pro Phorm. § 43, p. 955.

frequently the case with the chieftain of a German tribe, or Highland clan, and the tanaist of an Irish sept. In these latter cases, however, headship was to some extent elective, seldom travelling out of a single family, but often, for the better security of the tribe in barbarous and warlike times, passing over the infant son of the deceased chief in favour of his younger brother, on the system which has been described as "Keltic Primogeniture."* This was not indeed the only or the most important alteration in the form of Primogeniture, which the exigencies of uncivilised society produced. The representative of the family tended more and more to become the absolute owner of the property he protected. When the family grew into a tribe or sept, a larger portion of its land was gradually set apart as the private domain of its chief.† Of the spoil of conquest, when it took the shape of an increase in territory, he doubtless often secured for his personal advantage the largest share; it must frequently, indeed, have happened that he was the only person capable of employing it with profit. Since the publication of *Ancient Law*, it has generally been agreed that it was under some such circumstances as those indicated above, that the modern system of Primogeniture arose. "Nothing in law," however, as its author pointedly remarks, "springs entirely from a sense of convenience." Had it not been for the important representative prerogatives which archaic law and archaic religion had always conferred on the eldest son, his proprietary rights could scarcely have arisen during that period of confusion which accompanied the gradual dissolution of the Empire of the West.

Let me endeavour, before proceeding to the immediate history of our own law of succession to real property, briefly to sum up the most probable explanation of the circumstances and ideas under the immediate influence of which the modern system of Primogeniture arose. We first encounter it as the customary method of devolution among those beneficiaries who received grants of Roman provincial land on condition

* See Maine, *Early History of Institutions*, pp. 200—202; *Ancient Law*, pp. 239—242.
† *Early History of Institutions*, p. 204.

of military service, from Karl the Great and other Frankish chieftains.* These estates were the cradle of Feudalism; they also became the cradle of Primogeniture in its modern and Western form. Béstowed in the first instance for life, or merely during the grantor's pleasure, their history presents a very striking similarity to that of the Zemindaries under Muhammadan rule, which I have already sketched. A social state in Italy and other European countries, nearly the same as that in India, produced approximately the same results. The remoteness and feebleness of the central Government had a twofold effect. As the Musalman Governors gradually gave up their pretensions to appoint a new holder to every vacant zemindary as practically untenable, and contented themselves with a formal recognition of the representative of the deceased, so "the Benefice," as Sir Henry Maine expresses it, "gradually transformed itself into the hereditary Fief." Again, in either case, owing to the fact that each Zemindar and each chieftain had to look to himself alone for protection and defence, it was soon found desirable to secure the stability of the estate by perpetually vesting it in a single head. It would seem that the thoughts of men in a troubled and lawless period almost unconsciously reverted to a state of society which, as we have seen, must have once existed in both East and West. There had been a time when every family was a miniature State. The *paterfamilias* at that period not only exercised over his household the plenary authority of its political head, and representative to the outer world, but was also vested with full *proprietary* rights and their correlative duties. On his death his position, as a rule, devolved on the eldest male ascendant of the family, that is, in the usual course of events, on his eldest son. At a later epoch, when the family was absorbed in the State, and partitions of inheritance were authorised by law, the eldest born still maintained his quasi-political, and still more his religious, but almost entirely lost his proprietary prerogative. But at the time which we are now considering, when the State was

* *Ancient Law*, p. 229.

practically disintegrated into its original elements, but the original bonds of consanguinity had, with the disappearance of the ancient religion, lost a great measure of their force, the model which it seemed the most natural and convenient to follow was that which the earlier state of social life supplied. The main difference lay in the circumstance that while, for the sake of internal security, and as a means of protection against anarchy and violence, the proprietary *rights* of the eldest son were again called into existence, his correlative *obligations* were not equally revived. The law which, at a somewhat later date, was called in to determine his position, was the codified system of the latter days of the Roman Empire; and the application of its principles always tended to establish the plenary ownership of the holder of the fief. "The later Roman jurisprudence, like our own law, looked upon uncontrolled power over property as equivalent to ownership, and did not, and in fact could not, take notice of liabilities of such a kind, that the very conception of them belonged to a period anterior to regular law. The contact of the refined and the barbarous notion had inevitably for its effect the conversion of the eldest son into the legal proprietor of the inheritance. . . . . . The legal revolution was identical with that which occurred on a smaller scale, and in quite recent times, through the greater part of the Highlands of Scotland. When called in to determine the legal powers of the chieftain over the domains which gave sustenance to the clan, Scottish jurisprudence had long since passed the point at which it could take notice of the vague limitations on completeness of dominion imposed by the claims of the clansmen, and it was inevitable, therefore, that it should convert the patrimony of many into the estate of one."[*]

The narration of the circumstances under which the system of military tenure gradually superseded the old domainial form of property in Italy, and the ancient allod in Northern Europe—the history of the era of conditional alienations on the part of the larger, and more or less voluntary com-

[*] Maine, *Ancient Law*, pp. 238, 239.

mendations on that of the smaller proprietors—would scarcely be germane to our present subject. The growth of feudalism has been accounted for in many ways, and carefully discussed by many writers of ability On a subsequent page I shall endeavour briefly to elucidate its connection with Roman law. The advantages of tenure by military service to both lord and vassal must obviously, in troublous times, have been sufficiently considerable to account in great measure for its wide diffusion. It was an essential part of this system that the estates which were subject to it should be maintained at a considerable size, that each estate should contain a single individual responsible for the services attached to it, and that this individual should be of the male sex. Both for the feudal lord and for the tenant himself[*] partition was extremely dangerous and was everywhere discouraged. Hence there is little reason to be surprised at the rapidity with which the institution of Primogeniture, exactly suited as it was to the circumstances of the time, spread throughout Europe. After the Norman Conquest its diffusion over our own country was scarcely less swift; and it is here interesting to observe that one of the main reasons for the exceptional stability with which it has maintained its position in England lies in the fact of its having been unaffected among ourselves by the dissolving influence of that very legal system which had originally given it birth. As Primogeniture in Europe first arose from the application of the rules of Roman jurisprudence to a certain form of ownership, so one of its principal solvents on the Continent has been the recent and general adoption of legal principles of another kind, based on the *Code Napoléon*, and so ultimately on the Civil Law. In England, Primogeniture owed its introduction to other causes than that of the influence of Roman law, and has remained unimpaired by any later application of the Roman rules of succession.

[*] "The security of a landed estate, the protection which its owner could afford to those who dwelt on it, depended upon its greatness. To divide it was to ruin it, and to expose every part to be oppressed and swallowed up by the incursions of its neighbours."—Adam Smith, Wealth of Nations, p. 170; Ed., McCulloch.

Section II.—Primogeniture and Feudalism in England.

I ALLUDED, at the close of the last section, to the influence of Roman Law in determining the privileges and expanding the rights of the eldest son under the feudal system of tenure. It should also be observed that Roman Law—and especially the law which prevailed in the western portion of the Empire at the time of the invasion of the barbarians—had no small share in producing the institution of feudalism itself. One of the most characteristic features of that system lies in the doctrine of a double property in land held according to its rules, which it always involved. There were the rights of the superior lord, and the rights of his vassals; these latter, in turn, as the practice of subinfeudation became more frequent, acquired tenants of their own, often bound to render them service and fealty of a nature precisely similar to those which they themselves yielded to the grantor of the fief; and this is the form which, soon after the compilation of Domesday Book, Feudalism very generally assumed in England. The inferior, or paravail tenants, held their lands from the barons, and the barons, or mesne lords, were the grantees of the king. In any case, however, the phenomenon of at least two sets of rights in the soil necessarily presents itself in all benefices or fiefs; and the origin of such a conception must in all probability be traced, not to the rude and simple *Leges Barbarorum*, but to the institutions and laws of Rome. It has been supposed by some writers that this " duplication of proprietary right " was based on " the Roman distribution of rights over property into *Quiritarian*, or legal, and *Bonitarian*, or equitable."[*] There is much that is plausible in this opinion; and there is no doubt that the Roman element in Feudalism has been disparaged or neglected by writers who attributed too much to reasons of convenience which readily suggest themselves in explanation of almost any historical phenemenon, but which seldom account in a really satisfactory or adequate manner for its having occurred to

[*] *Ancient Law*, p. 295.

the intelligence of those among whom it first arose.* At the same time, the balance of probability disinclines us to believe that the Roman distinction between legal and equitable property—a distinction belonging to a decidedly advanced stage of juridical thought, and implying the regular operation of courts of law†—really actuated the substitution by the barbarians of feudal for allodial tenures; and this impression is confirmed by the fact that there was another form of ownership recognised by Roman law, and subsisting in the districts where its influence was first experienced by the barbarians, which it is much more natural to regard as the model after which the benefices were shaped. Sir Henry Maine has pointed out that while the *latifundia* of the Roman patricians were almost invariably cultivated by slave labour, large estates of the same kind when held, as was often the case, by the Municipalities were frequently let to free tenants. The Municipal corporations found the work of superintending slave gangs an uncongenial and unprofitable occupation; for the rapidity with which their functionaries were changed—only to be paralleled in modern times by the revolutionary proceedings of M. de Fourtou—made all effective control over such establishments impossible. The example of the Municipalities was eventually followed by many individual proprietors; and the equitable right of the tenant in the soil, originally determined by his contract with the proprietor, was ultimately recognised by the Prætor under the Greek designation of Emphyteusis. From the slave cultivators there arose in time the class of *coloni*, "formed partly," as Sir Henry considers, "by the elevation of the slaves, and partly by the degradation of the

---

* A somewhat different account of the origin of Feudalism is given by Professor Stubbs (Constitutional History of England, Vol. I. pp. 251, 252, note) as the result of "the recent investigations of German writers." He practically adopts in its entirety the theory of Waitz. But with regard to the recent investigations of German writers it is well to bear in mind the caution suggested by Sir Henry Maine :—"In later times a new source of error has been added to those already existing, in that pride of nationality which has led German writers to exaggerate the completeness of the social fabric which their forefathers had built up, before their appearance in the Roman world."—Ancient Law, p. 296.

† Ancient Law, p. 298.

free farmers;" just as he has in another work explained how the status of the inferior tenants of a fief in many cases formed a middle stage between the position of the free "peasant proprietors" of the præ-manorial village community, and that which was held by the villeins of the lord. The services of the *coloni* were of a base or predial character, and from the *coloni medietarii*—that is, those who paid as rent one-half of the produce of the land—arose the *metayer* tenantry of modern Europe. The general analogy between this system and the old English socage tenure is very obvious; but it would doubtless be rash to assume that there was any historical connection between them. Meanwhile, the Emphyteuta attained a much more honourable and secure position; his subordinate ownership was fully recognised by equity; and he was protected from ejectment so long as his quit-rent was regularly paid, and the other stipulations of his original covenant with the superior owner duly observed. It is here especially important to notice the still closer similarity to the system of benefices which Emphyteusis, in one of its branches, presented. The *agri limitrophi* by which the frontiers of the Empire on the Danube and the Rhine were preserved from incursions of the barbarians, were held of the State by veteran soldiers, often themselves of barbarous extraction, on terms similar to those enjoyed by the ordinary Emphyteuta; but instead of a quit-rent being required, the services imposed on them were only occasional, and exclusively military in their character. These grants of land usually descended to the heirs of the grantee, and, in the words of Sir Henry Maine, "it seems impossible to doubt that this was the precedent copied by the barbarian monarchs who founded feudalism."*

It may be regarded as certain that the feudal system was as unknown in the original abodes of the German conquerors of the Empire, as it was in England itself before the Norman invasion. The rapidity with which it spread in our own country must be mainly ascribed to the circumstances which, after the conquest, or, if the term be preferred, the

---

* The above sketch is epitomised from *Ancient Law*, pp. 295—303.

"acquisition" of England, led King William to parcel out so large a portion of the kingdom between those who had accompanied him in his expedition. As the nobility of the Thegns had superseded the more ancient nobility of the Eorls, so the Thegns themselves were in turn supplanted by William's Barons. But the Companions of the King, among the Norse folk, as in the polity of ancient Germany, and in that of ancient Ireland, appear to have held a position very inferior to that of the great allodial proprietors who remained at home on their paternal lands. Their relation to the chief they followed bore a close resemblance to that of the Roman client to his patron;* it is, perhaps, scarcely too much to describe their status as quasi-servile; and it is from this circumstance alone that we are able fully to understand some of the apparently degrading incidents of that "knight's service," which the proudest Norman Baron was bound to render to his liege.

Some difficulty has occasionally been felt at the use of two names—benefice and feud—for a system of tenure apparently in either case identical. The explanation appears to be that the fief was chronologically the later of the two; that the feudal tenant succeeded the beneficiary, and was endowed as a rule with ampler privileges. Sir Martin Wright, indeed, in his learned Introduction to the Law of Tenures, treats the words as synonymous, and quotes the definition of a benefice given in the Book of Feuds, namely, as a gift proceeding from the grantor's benevolence, of such a nature, that while the usufruct was on certain conditions assigned to the grantee, the property always remained with the donor.† It is known, however, that such gifts were at first precarious, being held originally at the will of the lord, subsequently from year to year, and afterwards for the tenant's life;‡ while it appears from a statement of

* See Maine, Ancient Law, pp. 229, 303; Early History of Institutions, pp. 145, 6; Freeman, Comparative Politics, p. 261.

† Quod ex benevolentia ita dabatur alicui ut proprietas rei penes dantem remaneret, ususfructus ad accipientem eiusq : hæredes pertinaret ad Hoc, Ut ille et eius hæredes Domino fideliter servirent. Feud. Lib. 2 ; Tit. 23.

‡ Wright, Law of Tenures, p. 14.

Muratori* that they sometimes held good only during the life of the *donor*, in which case they retained the name of benefices. Spelman in like manner affirms that such gifts, while dependent on the donor's pleasure, were known by the name of *munera*; that when held for a fixed term, as for life, they become *beneficia*; while they first received the name of *feuda* when they began to be granted for what was practically a perpetuity.† It may be taken as certain that the latter was the name by which these military tenures were ordinarily designated at the period when they were first introduced into this country.

The etymology of *feodum* has proved a fertile source of speculation. It has even been derived from Emphyteusis, while a Keltic origin, scarcely more plausible than the Greek, has recently been suggested by a writer on ancient Irish law, who connects the word with the well-known *fuidhir* tenantry of the Irish chiefs. Wright, after Somner, considers it a compound of "Feh, Feo, or Feoh" with "Hade, Head, or Hode, importing quality, kind, or nature," ‡ Feudum being therefore that which was held in Fee-hode. The first part, at all events, of this etymology is almost certainly correct. The Anglo-Saxon *feoh*, the old Norse *fé*, the modern German *vieh*, and the Latin *pecus*, are all obviously connected, and all originally denoted cattle. The importance and value of horned herds in early times are strikingly illustrated by the fact that, in several languages, from these words derivations were formed signifying property in general. *Pecunia* at once occurs to the mind; the modern *Capital* of political economy, and *Chattel* of the common law, had in all probability no other origin; while *Fee*, so important a word in the history of tenures, would seem to have been immediately formed from the old Teutonic words mentioned above, and to have been itself the parent of *Feod* or *Feud*.

* Antiquit. Ital. Med. Aev. dissert. 11.

† Posthumous Treatise of Feuds, 4, 6, 9. Similarly, Somner speaks of the Benefice as "elder brother of the Feud;" and affirms that the latter word was unknown till about 1000 A.D.—Treat. on Gavelkind, p. 112.

‡ Wright's Tenures, 4. Somner, Treatise of Gavelkind, 106-108; Spelman, Glossary ad verb. *Feodum*.

It has been much debated whether anything of the nature of feuds was known to our forefathers, before the "acquisition" of England by William the Conqueror. Dalrymple, in his essay on Feudal Property, endeavours to show that, under the Saxon rule, while much of the land remained allodial, a considerable proportion was held under conditions which were practically those of military tenure; and he adduces more than one weighty argument in support of his opinion that the feudal system, though elaborated and defined by the Normans, existed in germ or outline under the early English institutions.* The question is also discussed at length by Wright in the second chapter of his work; but the learned writer inclines to the belief that the main incidents of feudal tenure were unknown in this country until after the compilation of the Domesday record; while Lord Coke maintains that tenure by knight's-service existed, and even drew to itself the incidents of marriage, wardship, and relief, as early as the time of Ælfred. The contrary opinion has been maintained by, among others, Lord Hale, Somner, and Spelman; and the establishment of this view was indeed the main object with which the latter composed the elaborate treatise on the nature and origin of feuds, which was published after the writer's death by Bishop Gibson. †

There can at least be little doubt that the tenure of land in England previous to the conquest did not present any of those characteristics which afterwards so closely connected it with the law of Primogeniture. Our English forefathers

---

* So, also, on the whole, Professor Stubbs. "Domesday Book attests the existence in the time of Edward the Confessor of a large class of freemen who, by commendation, had placed themselves in the relation of dependence on a superior lord; whether any power of transferring their service still remained, or whether the protection which the commended freeman received from his lord extended so far as to give a feudal character to his tenure of land, cannot be certainly determined; but the very use of the term seems to imply that vassalage had not in these cases attained its full growth; the origin of the relation was in the act of the dependent. On the other hand, the occupation of the land of the greater owners by the tenants or dependents to whom it was granted by the lord prevailed on principles little changed from primitive times and incapable of much development."—Constitutional History, I., 188.

† See Wright, Tenures, p. 51.

were of course in no way insensible to the value of landed property; on the contrary, land, its produce, and the animals and instruments necessary for its cultivation were almost the only things of value with which they had much practical acquaintance;* and "land alone," in the words of a recent writer, "was recognised as the vehicle of all personal privilege and the basis of civil rank."† While the possession of land constituted the sole badge of freedom, and the one recognised claim to political representation, the "insolent prerogative" of the eldest son could scarcely be expected to exist. In point of fact, the early English law of inheritance shows considerable trace of the influence of the Roman law of succession, and in the event of intestacy the property of the deceased was divided among his children, or at all events among his sons, in equal portions. The custom of Gavelkind, so soon to be circumscribed within narrow territorial limits, at one time prevailed over the whole kingdom. Moreover the right of testamentary disposition, incompatible with the duty of a feudal tenant either to his lord or to his offspring, was fully recognised before the feudal era, the will employed being usually, as it would seem, of a nuncupative character; at the same time, there is no reason to suppose that this power was frequently exercised for the purpose of disinheriting the issue of the testator. Alienation *inter vivos* was of course equally permitted; and as lands were attachable to answer for their owner's debts, must sometimes have been of an involuntary kind. The restric-

* Sir James Stephen, in his *General View of the Criminal Law*, gives some striking instances of the insignificance, both in amount and value, of the "personal" property possessed by an English yoeman in early times. "In the 29th Edward I., a return was made of the personal property in Colchester and four adjacent townships, for the purpose of assessing a fifteenth; and it enumerates every article belonging to every person assessed, and almost all fall under one or other of these classes [cattle, agricultural produce, and household furniture]. . . . The amount of coined money is very small, especially when it is remembered that, as there were no banks, the money actually in a man's purse was all the money he had. The largest sums of ready money that I have noticed are 30s. in one case and 10s. in another—equivalent in purchasing power to £37 10s. and £12 10s. respectively."—Pp. 49-50.

† Systems of Land Tenure in Various Countries, p. 130: Mr. Wren Hoskyns, M.P.

tions on alienation which hampered the owner of a fief, whose interest was in fact a simple usufruct, must be afterwards considered; for the present it is sufficient to observe that they were unknown before the conquest. The Anglo-Saxon charters contained a full description of all landed property; and what were practically registers of deeds of transfer and assurance were carefully preserved. It is to the accuracy with which this duty was performed by his English predecessors that the facility and rapidity with which William procured the information contained in Domesday Book has been with much probability ascribed. It is also to be noticed that these registers, like the later record, had a public and military purpose. The most important branch of the *Trinoda Necessitas* was the military service to which every Thegn was bound, and which Professor Stubbs considers may probably be traced from the legislation of Ælfred.[*] Spelman regards this obligation as of a very systematic character, and as having extended over the whole kingdom; and he attributes to Ælfred the division of the country into tribes, with a view to the due apportionment of such services.[†] The exact relation between military duty and the tenure of property in the ante-Norman period is sketched by Mr. Stubbs, in a lucid and comprehensive manner, in a passage which I venture to transcribe:—

"In the obligation of military service may be found a second strong impulse towards a national feudalism. The host was originally the people in arms; the whole free population, whether landowners or dependents, their sons, servants, and tenants. Military service was a personal obligation; military organisation depended largely on tribal and family relations; in the process of conquest, land was the reward of service; the service was the obligation of freedom, of which the land was the outward and visible sign. But very early, as soon perhaps as the idea of separate property in land was developed, the military service became not indeed a burden upon the land, but a personal duty that practically depended on the tenure of land; it may be that

[*] Constitutional History, Vol. I., p. 191, cf., pp., 192-194.
[†] See Wright, Tenures, p 76.

every hide had to maintain its warrior; it is certain that every owner of land was obliged to the *fyrd* or *expeditio*; the owner of bockland as liable to the *trinoda necessitas* alone; the occupier of folkland as subject to that as well as to many other obligations from which bockland was exempted."*

The existence of such a system must have gone far to prepare the minds of the people for the changes which William introduced. In fact, as is remarked by an author with whom law students of the present day are abundantly familiar, "before the conquest, landowners were subject to military duties; and to a soldier it would matter little whether he fought by reason of tenure or for any other reason. The distinction between his services being annexed to his *land*, and their being annexed to the *tenure* of his land, would not strike him as very important."†

The general supercession of allodial by feudal tenures in England has been usually dated from the compilation of Domesday Book,‡ twenty years after the battle of Hastings, or Senlac; but the exact causes which led to the production of that work must remain uncertain. According to Blackstone, who bases his view on the Saxon Chronicle, the ancient military constitution of Ælfred having fallen into desuetude, the kingdom was inadequately protected against

* Constitutional History, Vol. I., pp. 189, 190.
† Joshua Williams, Law of Real Property, Twelfth Edition, p. 4.
‡ Professor Stubbs, however, considers that the feudal system, and the relation of lord and vassal which it involved, were generally in force before the Domesday Survey. With regard to the celebrated oath exacted at Salisbury, he observes :—" In this act has been seen the formal acceptance and date of the introduction of feudalism, but it has a very different meaning. The oath described is the oath of allegiance, combined with the act of homage, and obtained from all landowners, whoever their feudal lord might be. It is a measure of precaution taken against the disintegrating power of feudalism, providing a direct tie between the sovereign and all freeholders, which no inferior relation existing between them and the mesne lords, would justify them in breaking . . . The real importance of the passage as bearing on the date of the introduction of feudal tenure, is merely that it shews the system to have already become consolidated ; all the landowners of the kingdom had already become, somehow or other, vassals, either of the king, or of some tenant under him. The lesson may be learned from the fact of the Domesday survey."—Constitutional Hist. vol. i. pp. 266, 267.

foreign foes. An invasion was threatened by Denmark; and the King was compelled to summon to his aid a force of Normans from his Dukedom. In order to place the country in a posture of defence, and obviate the necessity of seeking in the future for extraneous aid, a Council was held, which resulted in the issue of the order for that historic survey.[*] It was completed without delay; the King convoked the principal landowners at Salisbury, received their homage and fealty, and distributed the land among them by a military and feudal tenure. It is uncertain how much of the land so divided was apportioned to Norman Barons, and how much still remained in the hands of English Thegns; to what extent, in fact, the distribution of Salisbury bore the aspect of a compulsory commendation of subjects hitherto more or less independent, or of a new grant to deserving beneficiaries. It is to be observed, however, that the amount of land in the hands of the King, and susceptible of fresh distribution, must during the previous twenty years have been constantly increasing. Those who had fought for Harold had forfeited their titles; there had been rebellions in the following years; Kent had revolted against the tyranny of Odo, and the Welsh princes had vainly endeavoured to break the Norman yoke; the House of Godwin had thrown off their allegiance, and been crushed, in 1068; Mercia and Northumbria had next taken up arms in a fruitless struggle; the fight for independence in which Eadwine and Morkeire fell had in 1071 reduced the Midland to submission; and the resistance of Hereward in the fens has acquired a romantic as well as an historical interest. Hence, in the words of our latest and, in some respects, ablest historian, "the desperate and universal resistance of his English subjects forced William to hold by the sword what the sword had won, and an army strong enough to crush at any moment a national revolt was necessary for the preservation of his throne. Such an army could only be maintained by a vast confiscation of the soil. The failure of the English risings cleared the way for its establishment; the greater

[*] Blackstone, 2 Comm. p. 48.

part of the high nobility had fallen in battle, or fled into exile, while the lower thegnhood had either forfeited the whole of their lands, or redeemed a portion of them by the surrender of the rest. We see the completeness of the confiscation in the vast estates which William was enabled to grant to his more powerful followers."*

From the point of view of the historian of the law of real property, one of the most important results of the new Constitution lay in the theory to which it gave birth, that all land in the kingdom, whatsoever its tenure, was held, mediately or immediately, of the king himself. As the sovereign is affirmed by the lawyers to be the fountain of all grace, so at the time of Domesday arose the doctrine that the Sovereign was lord paramount of the entire soil. A considerable proportion of the land was held by his tenants *in capite*, of whom there were fifteen hundred at the time of Domesday; and the obligations of service, homage and fealty, which the King imposed on his immediate vassals, were exacted by them as mesne lords with equal rigour from the paravail tenantry. As a general principle, it may be assumed that all lands granted by William on conditions of "frank-tenement" or *free-service* descended, on due performance of the original covenants, to the heirs of the grantee;† while those held by *knight's-service* descended exclusively to the eldest son. We know that this latter was not originally the case with socage lands, though socage was also a free tenure. The tenant in socage was allowed to alien by deed of feoffment at an early age; his land did not escheat in the event of attainder;‡ he was permitted a customary right of testamentary disposition; and on intestacy his estate, up to the reign of Henry II., when the devolution of socage land was assimilated, except in Kent,

---

* Green, Short History of the English People, p. 80.

† The hereditary character of benefices had been recognised by Charles the Bald, as early as 877 A.D.; and Professor Stubbs speaks of this as "rather a recognition of a presumptive right, than an authoritative enunciation of a principle." He regards it as "a clear proof of the generality of the usage."—Constitutional History, Vol. I., p. 254, note.

‡ Blackstone quotes the maxim, "The father to the bough, the son to the plough," referring, of course, to the accepted derivation of the word.

to that of estates held by military tenure, was equally divided among all the sons.* It has, indeed, been contended by some writers that fees held by knight's-service were not originally *feuda individua,* or indivisible, and that in the case of these lands also the law of Primogeniture was of somewhat later growth. The point is principally of antiquarian importance; but the probabilities of the matter are all the other way. Hale and Somner, for instance, point to the Constitution of the Emperor Frederick Barbarossa, establishing that principle of descent, seventy years subsequent to the date of Domesday; and they seem to think that it was only at that time that Primogeniture became general in our own country. But it is quite clear that any Constitution of Frederick could in England have had no other influence than that of a model; and it has been already shewn that a similar model was to be found in the customs which prevailed among the holders of benefices at a period considerably anterior to the Conquest. The establishment of *honorary* feuds, or feuds to which a title of nobility was attached, and which were necessarily unsusceptible of division, must doubtless have greatly contributed to the rapid spread of Primogeniture. In fact, if we examine with any care what we know to have been from the earliest time the characteristic incidents of knight's-service, we shall be led irresistibly to conclude, with both Wright and Blackstone, that they necessarily involved the descent of, at all events, the "capital fee" to the eldest son alone. To that examination I now proceed; after which it will be most convenient to consider the restraints on alienation, both during life and by will, which at first existed, and the manner in which, chiefly at the instance of the vassal, partly at that of the lord, in part, also, for the protection of the

* Cum quis Hæreditatem habens moriatur, siplures reliquerit filios, distinguitur utrum ille fuerit Miles, sive per feodum militare tenens, aut Liber Sokemannus ; Quia si miles fuerit, vel per militiam tenens, tunc secundum ius Regni Angliæ primogenitus filius patri succedit in totum, Ita quod nullus fratrum suorum partem inde de iure petere potest. Si vero fuerit Liber Sokemannus, tunc quidem dividetur hæreditas inter omnes filios quotquot sunt per partes æquales, si fuerit Socagium et id antiquitus divisum.—Glanvil, Lib. 7, cap. 3, p. 49, n.

creditors of the former, they were successively removed, until at length Primogeniture has become nothing more than a custom, and a custom which any owner of a freehold estate in possession, in fee simple, or in tail, who will take the trouble to make a will or execute a deed, is able to surmount.

Among the *aids* which were required from the feudal tenant, the most important and regular consisted of a contribution to the expenses incurred by his lord in making his eldest son a knight, and providing a marriage portion for his eldest daughter. It was in the interest as well of the king as lord paramount, as of the mesne lord that the former provision was established, in order that there might be no lack of duly qualified persons for the defence of the State, as well from internal disorder as from foreign foes. The obligation, however, was confined to the knighthood of the eldest son; and this might be regarded as in itself almost a sufficient proof that the latter alone succeeded to the tenure of the fief. In order that he might efficiently perform the duties attached to it, it was obviously necessary that he should receive an unincumbered inheritance; no portion for his sister was allowed to be charged upon the land; and his father, while tenant for life, possessing an income which was little more than sufficient for his ordinary expenditure, and which the nature of the life he led and the habits of his order precluded him from increasing, could seldom possess any funds applicable for that purpose. The inferior tenant, therefore, like the Roman client, was expected to tender his contribution; but there is no reason to imagine that the sum thus levied on each was in ordinary cases considerable, or oppressively burdensome. The scantiness of the portions of the daughters of landed proprietors, which is so often in the present day made the subject of adverse comment, must have been still more characteristic of early times; and the disproportion of the daughter's dowry to the property of the son afforded much less substantial reason for complaint as long as every knight was practically obliged to select his wife from the same class. Further aids, less justifiable in their object, were subsequently exacted, until the abuses which thence arose were partially redressed by King John's charter, and the *confirmatio chartarum* of Edward I.[*] The amount payable on the knighthood of the son, or the marriage of the daughter, was fixed at twenty shillings by the Statute of Westminster the First.[†]

The *relief* paid on entering upon the estate by the heir of a deceased tenant, was at first entirely arbitrary; so that an exorbitant relief was really tantamount to disinherison.[‡] Such a state of things could not long be tolerated, and the moderate composition fixed by William I., though not respected by his immediate successor, was restored by the charter of the first Henry. If the heir of a knight's fee, on his father's decease, had attained his majority, he succeeded at once to the estate on payment of a relief of 100s. *Prima seisina*—the right of the superior lord to a year's profits of the land—was confined to the king's tenants *in capite*, and originated in the theoretical right of the lord to enter and take seisin of the lands of his deceased vassal, in order to protect the estate until the heir claimed and received investiture.[§]

The right of *wardship* was no doubt based on the supposition that the heir, until he attained his majority, was incapable of performing the services of a knight, and strikingly illustrates the close connection which was held to subsist between the enjoyment of the profits of an estate, and the due performance of the conditions on which it was held. Indeed, if a youthful heir were made a knight during his father's lifetime, wardship did not arise; and as this could ordinarily be done when the heir had attained the age of fifteen, the remedy for the incidental grievances of wardship—of which we meet with so many instances in the proceedings of the Court of Wards under the Tudor and early Stuart kings—must frequently have resided in the tenant's hands.

The right of *maritagium* exercised by the superior lord

---

[*] St. 25 Edw. I., c. 5, 6. [†] St. 3 Edw. I., c. 36.
[‡] 2 Blackst. Com., pp. 65, seq. [§] 2 Blackst. Com., p. 66.

over his infant wards was doubtless the most oppressive incident of that condition, and the one which, in the case of *male* wards, it is most difficult to justify. So far from being simply employed in order to secure a trustworthy tenant or a suitable alliance, it was doubtless perverted and abused until it became an instrument of gross extortion. The right, however, was expressly recognised by the Statute of Merton ;* and only a tardy and unsatisfactory remedy was found in the invention of the doctrine of Uses, and the partial exemption subsequently conceded by the well-known Statute of Wills of Henry VIII.

Of all the incidents of knight's service, that which most closely connected it with the rule of Primogeniture, consisted in the *fines* which were levied on alienation of the land. Neither lord nor vassal could in early times break the feudal bond which subsisted between them, except by mutual consent. Considering the intimate character of the relation, and the almost domestic nature of some of the services which the tenant had agreed to render, it was thought unreasonable that he should be compelled to perform them to a stranger ;† and accordingly a new lord could not enter upon his predecessor's rights except on the voluntary attornment of the vassals. This restraint, however, did not long maintain its early rigidity; and the holder of a seignory or a reversion was permitted to convey his privileges by levying a fine, without the tenant's concurrence; while, as the result of this judicial process, attornment could be compelled, until a statute of Anne rendered it no longer necessary.‡ The tenant's liberty of alienating seems to have been of slower growth; the fine demanded on such an event did not, like the relief exacted from his heir, almost immediately become a moderate composition of fixed amount, but seems to have entirely depended on the pleasure of the lord. Even after the passing of *quia emptores*, the king's tenants *in capite* were unable to alien without a licence, the price of

* St. 20 Hen. III., c. 6.
† Wright, Tenures, pp. 30, 31.
‡ St. 4 & 5 Anne, c. 16, s. 9. See Williams, Real Property, pp. 237, 238, 310.

which was fixed by a subsequent statute at a third of the annual value of the estate.*

Owing to this incident of tenure, the real or supposed interest of the lord tended greatly to secure the succession of the heir, and maintain the custom of Primogeniture. Before tracing the steps by which the right of alienation against both lord and heir was gradually acquired, it should be remarked that the last incident of tenure by knight's service—that of escheat—also contributed to the same end. The lord's reversionary interest must have increased his jealousy of any proceedings of the tenant, such as clandestine alienation or division, which might diminish the chance of its accruing, and enhanced the natural desire of the tenant to procure for himself a duly qualified heir, according to the conditions of his tenure.

The keen objection to alienation by his tenant which the feudal lord experienced, was a natural consequence of the feudal system, and particularly of that form of it which was introduced into England by the policy of the Conqueror. The mesne lord, including the tenant *in capite*, was himself held to a strict performance of services by his superior; and his capacity for rendering them was liable to be seriously endangered by an excessive multiplication of the number of his tenants. Thus a feeling similar to that which tended to keep estates in the hands of the same family prescribed their unincumbered devolution to a single heir. The land began to be regarded less as a means of subsistence than as a security for defence; and if a tenant were permitted to divide his estate among his creditors or his kin, its efficiency in this respect was seriously diminished. The holder of a knight's fee was bound to serve his sovereign for forty days in the year, and to furnish his equipment at his own expense; but those who held only a portion of a fee were only required to serve for a proportionate time. "Hence the splitting of feuds had the effect of inconveniently increasing the number of the forces at the commencement of a campaign, and of so limiting the duration of their service,

---

* St. 1 Edw. III., c. 12.

that they became useless for anything, unless it might be attempted by a *coup de main*. The quality of the feudal militia was also much deteriorated by the subdivision of fiefs; the holders of small portions not being able to furnish a completely equipped horseman even for the shortest period."*

The utility of the system of Primogeniture from a military and defensive point of view is indeed extremely obvious, and would probably in itself sufficiently account for the stability which it acquired among English institutions. It would seem, however, that it really could claim to possess other advantages, considered as a means of agricultural and economical improvement, which have been very generally neglected or ignored. There can be no doubt that previous to the supercession of the old allodial system and the custom of gavelkind by feudal tenures and the rule of Primogeniture, there existed in this country large tracts of waste or untilled land which only needed reclamation, and enormous forests which urgently required a vigorous application of the axe. But the organisation of society under our English forefathers was such as to render any general scheme for the extension of the area of cultivated and productive land almost entirely impracticable. The manor, when the feudal system was introduced, was in most cases superimposed on a præ-manorial village community; and when society is grouped in village communities, agricultural progress is difficult in the extreme. Custom presses on the co-proprietors with obligatory force; obsolete methods of cultivation are adhered to with strange tenacity; individual enterprise is discouraged by a system in which all alike participate in the fruits of the superior industry or sagacity of a single member of the group; and anything resembling capital is of course entirely unknown. When land is held in this manner, any great change in the manner of employing it can seldom be immediately profitable to its proprietors; even if it is, it is very difficult to prove its lucrative character to those

* Lyttelton, Henry II., vol. iii. 83-92: quoted by McCulloch, p. 25.

with whom its adoption rests; and even if the advantage of such alteration can be demonstrated to the satisfaction of the most ignorant and prejudiced—who will probably possess a right of vetoing any change which their more intelligent neighbours may advocate—it by no means follows that they will be able to free themselves from the immaterial fetters which have been riveted by uninterrupted usage, and proceed to carry it into effect. The hopelessness of expecting any advanced agricultural science under such conditions may be illustrated by the working of the Russian Mir, or village community, of the present day. In the Mir the lands are periodically redistributed among the peasant owners. The cultivation is of the most rude and primitive kind; and unless the conditions are greatly changed, it seems likely to defy all efforts at improvement.* The comparative poverty and unproductiveness of land in Russia is probably to be attributed almost as much to these circumstances as to any obstacles which barrenness of soil or inclemency of climate may engender; and the disastrous effect of every system of joint-ownership with which we are acquainted on the individual enterprise and economical progress of the proprietors, seems in itself to supply a weighty argument against many of the communistic theories of modern times. For the early rescue of England from an equally wretched economical condition, we are probably in great measure indebted to the feudal system. The feudal lord was hampered by no effete agricultural customs; he was able to make the most of his estate according to the best advice procurable at the time; he commanded sufficient labour to reclaim, by the aid of his villeins, the waste land, which was always under his immediate control; and, most important of all, he was often in a position to sacrifice immediate returns for an assured advantage in the future, of which he knew that his heir, at all events, would reap the benefit. The same results appear to have at one time

* See Mr. Wallace's valuable paper on the Russian Mir, in *Macmillan's Magazine*, June, 1876; and the chapters in which he more fully explains the system of land-tenure in his work on Russia. Compare also *Systems of Land-Tenure*, pp. 404, 405.

followed from the tenure of large tracts of land by the Zemindars in Orissa and Bengal,* with whom, as has already been noticed, alone among Indian proprietors, descent according to the rule of Primogeniture prevailed.

And yet in England many of the inferior tenants must have retained a traditional recollection of the period before the Conquest, when they were free to alienate their lands, and dispose of them as they thought best, with no other restraints than those imposed by prudence and family affection. When the personal attendance of the feudal tenants began to be commuted into escuage or scutage money—first taken, according to Blackstone, on the occasion of Henry II.'s expedition to Toulouse—all the advantages of that system of tenure seemed to many to be lost, and nothing but the oppressive nature of its incidents to remain. Before this, however, the tenant of a freehold estate of inheritance had made some progress towards acquiring the right to dispose of it during his life; and, as far as it is possible to judge, from the earliest introduction of the feudal system into England the grant of an estate for the tenant's own life alone was the exception rather than the rule. At first, however, a gift to a man and his heirs was construed to exclude all but lineal descendants, so that it had the same effect as that subsequently produced by the addition of the words, "of his body," to the deed of feoffment; and this construction was only obviated by the gift of estates to be held on the theory of *feudum novum ut antiquum*. Thus collateral heirs were at first admitted by a legal fiction; hence, too, arose the anomalous rule by which a father was, until less than half a century ago, in all cases excluded from inheriting his son's estate; and on this principle the whole tenure of fee-simple estates, and the method of their devolution on intestacy depended, until at the date referred to important changes were introduced into the law of inheritance.†

While the right to alienate, in the strict sense of the word,

* Maine, *Village Communities*, p. 163. The foregoing paragraph was in part suggested by pp. 160-165 of the same work.
† St. 3 & 4 Will. IV., c. 106.

was only very gradually acquired, after a severe and protracted struggle, that of subinfeudation seems to have been recognised in the earliest period of feudal tenures as an integral part of the feudal system. The tenant was not allowed to transfer the land together with its incidental services; but he was permitted to "sub-let" it on such terms, that he himself received from the paravail occupant services sufficient to enable him to himself perform those due to the superior lord.* The mischiefs, however, involved in the subdivision of fiefs, which formed the main justification of the rule of Primogeniture, and of the restraints by which direct alienation was checked, were scarcely less palpable when the occupancy of the soil was transferred by this process. We find, accordingly, that the Crown tenants *in capite* were not permitted to employ it; while, with regard to others, considerable restrictions were imposed both on the purposes for which it might be resorted to, and the quantity and nature of the land which might be thus conveyed. It appears from the law of Henry I., which has been already cited, that subinfeudation of hereditary "Bocland" was prohibited; and Glanvil, writing about a generation later, after mentioning the special objects for which subinfeudation was favoured by the law, adds that only "a reasonable part" of the estate might be diverted in that manner.† So vague a rule can have afforded but scanty protection to the feudal lord. The tenant often failed to render his services satisfactorily, owing to the default of

* Though Subinfeudation (by which a new inferior Feud was carved out of the old, the old one still subsisting) was allowed by the Feudal Law, yet Alienation (by which the original Feud itself was transferred, and a new Feudatory substituted in the place of the old) was not. . . . . . It is clear that Subinfeudations were warranted by the Feudal Law, and that they were an original and necessary branch of the feudal policy itself.—Wright, Tenures, pp. 156, note *a;* 159, note *h*.

† Licet autem ita generaliter cuilibet de terra sua *rationabilem partem* pro sua voluntate cuicunque voluerit libere in vita sua *donare*.—Liv. 7, c. 1. He is speaking, it should be noticed, of Subinfeudation, not Alienation, the word *dono* being used, which always before *quia emptores* created a tenure between feoffor and feoffee. . . . . . Tenentur autem Hæredes Donatorum *Donationes* et res *Donatas*, sicut *rationabiliter* factæ sunt, illis quibus factæ sunt et hæredibus suis Warrantizare.—*Ibid*, c. 2. It need scarcely be observed that Glanvil here clearly uses the reflexive *suis* incorrectly for *eorum*.

those to whom he had transferred a portion of his interest; while the other incidents of his tenure, in their nature scarcely susceptible of transfer or apportionment—the rights of wardship, marriage, and escheat—were sometimes entirely lost to the superior. It is therefore not surprising that the barons made vigorous and persistent efforts to check a practice so disadvantageous to themselves; it was not, however, prohibited by Magna Charta; but on the revision and renewed promulgation of the Charter, at the instance of Langton and the barons, a provision was inserted forbidding any tenant to dispose of his land by subinfeudation, without reserving a portion sufficient in itself to answer the requirements of his lord.* Even this restriction, however, in the end proved insufficient; and at length the power of subinfeudation was entirely and finally abolished by the famous statute of Edward I., of which the preamble begins with the words *quia emptores terrarum,* and which accordingly is usually cited under the title of *Quia emptores.*† By this statute, every tenant of an estate in fee simple—with the exception of the king's tenants *in capite,* who did not acquire equal liberty until the reign of Edward III.‡— acquired full power to alienate his estate during his lifetime (the right of *testamentary* disposition was not conceded until late in the reign of Henry VIII., and then only to the extent of two-thirds of the land, in cases where it was held by knight's-service§), on condition, however, that the alienee should hold not of the previous tenant, but of the original grantor or his representative, and on such conditions and subject to such services as had formerly been attached to the occupancy of the estate.

It will appear from the foregoing summary that the rights of the heir must have been to a great extent preserved by the restrictions on subinfeudation successively imposed in

* Nullus Liber Homo *det* de cætero amplius alicui quam ut *de residuo terræ* possit sufficienter fieri Domino Feodi servitium ei debitum.—Cap. 32. See Wright, Tenures, pp. 157, 158; 2 Blackst. Comm., pp. 90, 91.

† St. 18 Edw. I., c. 1.

‡ St. 1 Edw. III., c. 12. Compare Wright, Tenures, pp. 162-167.

§ St. 32 Hen. VIII., c. 1; and 34 & 35 Hen. VIII., c. 5.

the interest of the superior lord. It is remarkable, however, that it was precisely in those cases in which the heir was most likely to be injured by the practice, that subinfeudation was especially favoured by early feudal law. As a rule he was not likely to suffer any graver injury from the process than is experienced in modern times by an expectant tenant in tail from leases granted or conveyances effected by a life tenant in possession under the settled estates Act. It is not to be supposed that the feudal tenant was habitually generous for nothing, or that he underlet his land without a fair equivalent; and at a time when ready money was extremely rare, and there were no merchant princes eager to acquire the ancestral acres of impoverished men of birth, absolute sales for ready money paid down, or even anything of the nature of modern mortgages, must have been of extremely rare occurrence. Thus subinfeudation generally assumed the form of perpetual leases, for which services or rents fairly proportioned to the value of the land were of course expected.* The incoming tenant would rarely have had the power to pay, even if the grantor had the ingenuity to demand, anything like an exorbitant "fine" for the privilege of occupying the land on terms which did not represent its real value; and it is natural to suppose that a tenant, if only for his own sake, in transferring a portion of his estate, did not fail to impose such conditions as common prudence would dictate; while the heir of course succeeded to the services which his father had required. But the cases of subinfeudation above referred to were of a somewhat different kind. They arose from the peculiar forms of tenure known as *frank-marriage* and *frankalmoign*; and it appears from a passage in Glanvil, that subinfeudation for these objects was recognised as peculiarly deserving of encouragement and protection.† In the former case the daughter, in whose

* Williams, Real Property, pp. 36, 37.

† Potest quilibet Liber Homo terram habens quandam partem terræ suæ cum filia sua, vel cum alia qualibet muliere, *dare* in Maritagium . . . Quilibet etiam cuicunque voluerit potest *dare* quandam partem sui liberi tenementi . . . loco religioso in Eleemosynam. Glanv. Lib. 7, c. 1. It is perhaps allowable to conjecture that the clause *vel cum alia qualibet muliere* is intended to cover the case of a mesne lord who wished to create such a tenure on the marriage of a younger son.

interest the conveyance was effected, and her husband, held the land so granted to them and their heirs free from all manner of service, with the exception of an oath of fealty, until the fourth degree of consanguinity from the donor was passed; while grantees in *frankalmoign*—usually religious houses or corporations—were free for ever from any kind of temporal service.* The recognition of such grants was doubtless due to the authority of the Church, and must clearly have been always liable to grave abuse; and the unjustifiable encroachments on the rights and expectations both of the heir and the superior lord which thence arose, soon gave rise to stringent enactments enforcing the necessity of licences in mortmain for all such conveyances—enactments, however, which ecclesiastical ingenuity was constantly successful in evading, and which eventually produced the elaborate system of conveyances to *use*, which flourished under the protection of the ecclesiastically administered equity-courts.†

The free right of *alienation*, as the indefeasable prerogative of every tenant of an unconditioned fee, was definitively established by *Quia emptores*; as has been observed above, the steps by which it was acquired were extremely gradual; and the concession was only finally made, partly because the barons had begun to see that it was less injurious to their interests than the alternative practice of subinfeudation, of which I have traced the history, partly because the policy of Edward I. was distinctly adverse to the more illiberal of the restrictions which feudalism had imposed. The first advance in this direction seems to have been made by the seventieth law of Henry I., which, while maintaining the inalienable character of Bockland, expressly allowed every free man to dispose as he pleased of lands he had himself acquired.‡ If, however, his whole property consisted in acquisitions he was not permitted, we are informed by

* Williams, Real Property, pp. 36, 37.
† 2 Blackst. Comm. 268-272.
‡ *Vide* p. 12, *supra*.

Glanvil, to entirely disinherit the heir-at-law.* The next step, according to Blackstone, was the concession of full liberty to alienate in the case of lands purchased by a man "to himself and his assigns;" and, apparently at the same time, it was decided that one-fourth of the ancestral estate might be conveyed away without the consent or priority of the heir; a provision which it may be conjectured was first evoked at the instance of the clergy, or possibly of creditors at a time when bonds of specialty were not in general use, and the obligation of the heir to satisfy his father's debts was very undefined. It seems to have been shortly after this that, as the tenants gradually became stronger, less willing to accept land under the old strict conditions, of which accumulated experience had already demonstrated the burden and abuse, and more determined to recover the freedom of alienation their English predecessors had enjoyed, the form of feoffment came into general use, by which estates were conveyed to the purchaser, his heirs, or *whomsoever he might assign;* and the livery of seisin on such conditions involved at first full liberty, as well of alienation as of subinfeudation. It was during the reign of Henry III., from whose irresolute administration the barons succeeded in extorting many concessions which his son, though a man of very different calibre, was unable and perhaps unwilling to annul, that feoffments of this character began to furnish the rule by which all grants were construed;† and even in the case of estates limited, not merely to a man "and his heirs," but to the purchaser "and the heirs of his body," it was held that the tenant had full liberty to alienate immediately on the birth of issue. The heir, it was laid down, had no legal claim on the gift made to his ancestor; his birth was simply the condition which rendered it absolute; *nihil acquirit,* writes Bracton, *ex donatione facta antecessori, quia cum donatorio non est feoffatus.* The fee-simple, it was held,

* Si *questum tantum* habuerit is qui partem terræ suæ *donare* voluerit, tunc quidem hoc ei licet: sed non totum questum, quia *non potest filium suum hæredem* exhæredare.—Glanvil, Lib. 7, c. 1.

† Williams, Real Property, p. 38.

vested from the beginning, subject only to the reversion to the grantor on the event of the grantee dying without issue;[*] and if he had issue, and suffered the conditional fee to descend to the heir, the latter might immediately convey it away.[†] It is clear that when all grants began to be construed in this manner the heir's rights were in theory gravely imperilled; practically, as will appear from what has been said above, they were in no great danger except from those eleemosynary grants, frequently induced by superstitious terror, which law constantly prohibited and equity as constantly protected; but Primogeniture had been for the time reduced to a custom, and rested on the more or less precarious footing of established precedent, social feeling, and economical convenience. The encroachments on the feudal privileges of the superior lord were, however, of a more direct and serious character; the alienations which domestic interests must frequently have dictated to the tenant diminished the value of his services in much the same way as the as yet unchecked practice of subinfeudation; while the chance of a reversion, at one time considerable, had become practically infinitesimal. It was for these reasons that the barons, five years before *Quia emptores* had established the unfettered power of alienating estates held in fee simple, procured the enactment of the celebrated statute *De Donis Conditionalibus*,[‡] which effectually protected both the remainder of the heir and the reversion of the lord in estates granted to the tenant and the heirs of his body. The form of the gift and the intention of the donor were for the future to determine the devolution of the land; and *feodum talliatum*, the offspring of *De donis*,[§] restored in all its pristine strictness the birth-right of the eldest son. For nearly one hundred and seventy years the law of Primogeniture prevailed in all its strictness over most of the landed property in England, by means of estates tail which it was impossible for the

[*] Willion *v.* Berkley, Plowd, 233.
[†] Nevil's case, 7 Rep., 124.
[‡] St. 13 Edw. I., c. 1.
[§] "Littleton tells us that tenant in fee-tail is by virtue of the Statute of Westminster the Second."—2 Blackst. Comm., 112.

tenant in possession either to alienate during life or control by any posthumous testament; and it therefore seems advisable, before proceeding further with that portion of the history of English land-law which is connected with the present subject, to sketch the origin and history of this peculiar system of tenure from its first introduction at Rome to its later course in modern Europe.

Section III.—The History of Entails.

The assertion of Gibbon, adopted by Adam Smith, that entails were unknown to the Roman law, has been successfully questioned by more recent writers, and particularly by McCulloch.* It is true that the system of tying up estates by means of settlements is of quite modern origin; but the Roman proprietor of the Imperial period was protected by the Prætor in his efforts to prescribe the devolution of his property through more than one generation by creating a series of life interests and remainders. It has, however, been incorrectly supposed, doubtless owing to the signification of the word in French property law, that the *vulgar* or *pupillar* substitutions, with which students of Roman law are familiar, were of the nature of entails. The former, however, was merely the substitution of another heir in the event of the one first named declining the inheritance, or dying, or becoming disqualified during the testator's lifetime, the object, of course, being to avoid the danger of accidental intestacy. In the latter case, a second heir was named on whom the property should devolve in the event of an infant heir dying while disqualified by minority from making a will. In neither instance was any exceptional restraint imposed on alienation. The origin of entails must rather be sought in the military testament, which was made under peculiar conditions, and by which the testator was permitted to control the posthumous devolution of his property to an extent not then conceded to the civilian.† The heir, under a testament so executed, might be confined to a life interest, and another substituted to whom the property was to go on

---

* Treatise on Succession, pp. 44, 45.

† Montesquieu says that the military will "ne fut établi que par les constitutions des empereurs; ce fut une de leurs cajoleries envers les soldats." (Bk. xxvii.) This of course is a mistake; such wills were recognised comparatively early in the republican period; we find Cicero, for instance, mentioning the fact that in recent times many such wills had been invalidated owing to the change by which the armies were commanded, not by the consuls *auspicato*, but by proconsuls who did not hold the auspices; *ex quo*, he says, *in procinctu testamenta perierunt.*—De Nat. Deorum, ii. 9. The privileges, however, referred to in the text are of course to be assigned to the imperial age.

its expiration. Wills of this kind doubtless suggested the idea of utilising the method of devising on trust, or by *fidei-commissa*—originally invented to elude the provisions of the Voconian law—for a similar purpose. Trusts of the ordinary description were called *express*; and under them the *fiduciarius* had no more beneficial enjoyment of the property than an English trustee; but sometimes the testator* commanded him to enjoy the property for his own life, and to bequeath it to a person named in the original testament; such trusts were entitled *tacit*. The fiduciary heir was generally required to leave the property to such person as, at his demise, should be his own heir, according to the law of intestacy, or, sometimes, the heir of the original testator. The fiduciary had strictly a life interest; he was not permitted to alien the estate during his lifetime; and he could not dispose of it after his death otherwise than according to the instructions he had received. It would seem that at one time it was possible to create a series of life-estates in the foregoing manner;† but the policy of Justinian "abhorred perpetuities;" their inconvenient effects probably had been soon experienced; and the 159th Novel decreed that the appointed heir of a tacit fiduciary should receive the property untrammelled by any similar restrictions.‡

Gibbon speaks of the trust substitutions of French law as "a feudal idea grafted on the Roman jurisprudence." In France, as in England after the enactment of *De Donis*, and for a much longer period, it was permitted by instruments of this kind to tie up property for any number of lives. Every

---

* *Testator fidei-committens.*

† McCulloch cites the following specimen of a Roman entail, as "remarkable for its brevity, comprehensiveness, and distinctness":—*Volo meas œdes non vendi ab hæredibus meis neque fœnerari super eas; sed manere eas firmas simplices meis filiis et nepotibus universum tempus. Si autem aliquis eorum voluerit vendere partem suam, vel frenerari super eam, potestatem habeat vendere cohæredi suo, et fœnerari ab eo; si autem aliquis præter hæc fixerit, erit quod obligatur inutile atque irritum.* (Digest. Lib. xxxi. c. 88 15.)

‡ *Restitutiones fidei-commissæ usque ad unum gradum consistant.* The foregoing explanation of the Roman law of entails is abridged from a very lucid exposition in an article in the *Westminster Review*, October, 1824, the writer of which a paragraph in Mr. Mill's Autobiography permits me to identify with John Austin.

possessor of the estate was *grevé de substitution* to transmit it to the person who, according to the arrangement prescribed by the founder, might be entitled to succeed him. It was not until 1560 that by the Ordonnance d'Orléans, which has been attributed to Chancellor de l'Hôpital, such substitutions were limited to the third degree, reckoned inclusively from the author of the trust. This enactment was confirmed six years later by the Ordonnance de Moulins, which also limited entails previously instituted to the fourth degree. Matters continued on this footing until 1792, when substitutions and entails were entirely prohibited. The sentiments subsequently formulated in Proudhon's axiom, *La propriété c'est le vol*, were at that time extremely popular; and the legists doubtless believed that by abolishing trust estates they would be employing the surest means of carrying out the view of the revolutionists, and abolishing so objectionable an institution. By the *Code Napoléon* substitutions were indeed restored, but confined within such narrow limits as to make them practically powerless for good or ill. The *légitime* was strictly exempted from their operation; and while it was allowed to create life interests in the *disposable* portion of the property, they were only permitted if made in favour of the testator's own children, while the legatee was himself *grevé de restitution*, commanded, that is, to bequeath the whole of the property so acquired to *his* children in equal shares.*

Having thus briefly sketched the history of trust substitutions in Roman and French law, I return to the consideration of the very different fortune which, since the statute of Westminster the Second, the system of entailing—on which Primogeniture from that time mainly depended—has enjoyed in England. There is not, at least within the knowledge of the present writer, any available information as to the precise proportion that the land which fell under the provisions of *De Donis*, which prohibited, bore to the land which was affected by *Quia emptores* which, passed only five years after-

---

* The object of this regulation appears to have been to enable a testator, who wished to benefit the *children* of a son whom he distrusted, to make the latter a sort of *fiduciarius*.

wards, may be said to have encouraged alienation. It is probable, however, that the language of Blackstone and other writers has produced an impression that a greater extent of landed property was held in strict entail than was actually the case.* The later statute, we know, was passed at the instance and for the convenience of the barons, many of whom must have held estates unaffected by the preceding enactment—a circumstance which doubtless increased the dissatisfaction of others when they began to experience the evil effects which a system of perpetual entails must inevitably produce. We know moreover that large grants

* Thus Mr. Neate, formerly Professor of Political Economy at Oxford, in a lecture delivered in that University in 1859, speaks of the right to alien having been taken away from the great majority of proprietors by this statute:—" By this statute, then, the power of alienation, though recognised the more readily perhaps on this account by the later statute of *Quia emptores, was effectually taken away from the greater part of the lands of this country*, assuming, as we may safely do, that the greater part of the land, as certainly by far the greater part of the lordships did, belonged either to the nobility or to men sufficiently rich to desire either to found or to perpetuate a family. A further inducement to entail lands—and in those times of civil war it was a very powerful inducement—was that entailed lands in the hands of the heir were exempted from forfeiture even in the case of high treason." Two lectures on the History and Conditions of Landed Property, p. 28: by Charles Neate, M.A., Fellow of Oriel College. Oxford and London, J.H. and J. Parker, 1860.—It appears, however, from a pamphlet published five years later by the same author that he subsequently saw reason to greatly modify the opinion contained in the above passage. "This statute," he says, "is spoken of in Blackstone as a family law, and we are thereby led to suppose that the land of the country was generally brought under the fetters of entail by means of it. But *this was very far from being the case. Whatever may have been the reason of the statute, its importance and effects have been greatly overstated.* The Great Lords who passed the statute had probably no thought of diminishing their power over their demesne lands by entailing them upon their sons, and if they wished to do so they could not do it without resigning the immediate ownership. In those days there could be no will of land, and the simplicity of the law knew of no means by which a man who had the fee simple in possession could dispose of the reversion of his estate, reserving to himself the enjoyment for life. No doubt it frequently, or perhaps generally, happened that many granted a portion of their estates as an immediate provision for a son or daughter upon marriage, and this was done by a very simple and common form of entail. But men were not likely to grant the whole, or even the greater part of their property in this way, and there is abundant proof that *a very large portion of the land of the country was free from the restriction of entail*, and that the lords and owners of estates continued very generally to enjoy and to exercise the feudal liberty of alienation."—The History and Uses of the Law of Entail and Settlement, by C. Neate, M.A., M.P. London: Ridgway, 1865.

of land were constantly being made under the Plantagenet kings for religious and charitable purposes; with a single exception, every college in this University, of which there is scarcely one which does not in great part owe its existence to munificent donations of landed property by private benefactors, was founded subsequently to *De donis*; no less than seven colleges in Cambridge, and the same number at Oxford, date from the period when it was impossible to bar the heir's succession to any portion of an entailed estate; and it is a legitimate inference from this circumstance, that the quantity of land held in fee-simple must have always been very considerable. Moreover, it was in the reign of Edward III. that the doctrine of Uses was first developed; as a transfer of the use involved also a conveyance of the legal estate, they cannot have been applied to estates tail till several generations afterwards; and yet we know their diffusion through the whole land to have been extremely rapid, so much so indeed that as early as the succeeding reign the questionable character of some of these transactions called for legislative interference.* At the same time, notwithstanding all these considerations, the effects of *De donis* in restricting alienation must have been very widely felt; and for the grievous consequences which it from time to time produced, a remedy was long sought in vain.

The sketch of these consequences given by Blackstone†— who himself bases his description on a passage in Bacon's Treatise on the Use of the Law—is too well known to require more than the briefest allusion here. The injurious effect on the character of the eldest son, brought about by the certainty of succession, seems to have quickly become palpable. Fathers complained of disobedience and indolence, of vicious habits, wastefulness, and self-indulgence which, having no substantial means of marking their displeasure, they were powerless to correct; while the hardship of being unable, even with the consent of the eldest, to make any suitable provision for the younger children must

* St. 15 Rich. II. c. 5.   † 2 Blackst. Com. 116.

have been severely felt. The pecuniary position of the tenant in possession was also greatly prejudiced; for while leases for terms were unknown, the landlord could not sub-let to advantage; no tenant would pay a fine for the privilege of a precarious possession which the demise of the lessor might at any moment terminate; and while the tenant for life was sometimes unwilling and almost always unable, the occupier was still more reluctant and nearly equally powerless to effect any substantial improvements, however urgently required, of which the former could not bequeath the fruit or the latter feel assured of the enjoyment. All the objections, in fact, which, despite much recent legislation, are still urged against modern settlements, as deterring the expenditure of capital on the land, applied with ten-fold force to a system of perpetual entails, suddenly introduced at a period in many respects progressive. The state of the law pressed hardly on other classes than the owners of land; it often defrauded creditors and intending purchasers of what was rightly theirs. The heir, unless bound by specialty, was free, according as his honour or his judgment dictated, to pay or to repudiate the debts which his ancestor had incurred; and it was not until the reign of Henry VIII. that the heir to an entailed estate was rendered liable even to Crown debts, and then only to those secured by *judgment*.* The spirit of the common law may indeed be inferred from the circumstance that, until little more than twenty years ago, when a more equitable enactment was passed on the initiative of a private member,† the *personal* estate of a deceased intestate was, if sufficient for the purpose, exclusively liable for the satisfaction of his mortgage debts, while the realty descended unincumbered to the heir-at-law. Purchasers also, in the period subsequent to *de donis*, were often cruelly wronged by the production of latent entails which deprived them of land they had duly paid for, and of which they had done their utmost to ascertain the validity of the title. We are

* St. 33 Hen. VIII., c. 39, s. 75.

† St. 17 & 18 Vict., c. 113 (Mr. Locke King's Act); see, also, St. 30 & 31 Vict., c. 69.

told, moreover, that the tenant for life became "less fearful to commit murthers, felonies, treasons, and manslaughters,"* since entailed estates were not liable to forfeiture, and the consequences of his personal offence could not be visited on his heir; while the Crown itself was prejudiced by the statute, which greatly diminished its security for debts due from subjects whose property came under its provisions; so that "the King could not safely commit any office of account to such whose lands were entailed, nor other men trust them with loan of money."†

It certainly speaks volumes for the value attached to a law which placed the prerogative of the eldest son beyond the parent's control, and which maintained the principle of hereditary succession to ancestral property in all its strictness, that, from the day when *De donis* received the royal assent, neither king, nor barons, nor commons introduced any legislative proposal for its modification. The method by which in 1473 entails were for the first time barred, and the expectation of the heir defeated, was, as is well known, the result not of an enactment by the Parliament but of a decision of the judges. The device resorted to in Taltarum's case has been stigmatised by writers who do not affect to deny the generally beneficial nature of its consequences as a piece of "legal legerdemain;" but on the whole it seems somewhat remarkable that so commonplace and obvious a proceeding as a collusive recovery—for which the Roman *cessio in iure* furnished an almost exact precedent—was not long previously discovered by legal ingenuity. For it is to be noticed that this method of getting rid of his fetters was as open to the tenant in the time of the early Plantagenets as in that of the fourth Edward. The tenant in tail had never been exempted from the duty of defending his title in a court of law; and if he intentionally and deliberately failed to do so, his heir was entirely without redress. The case, it is true, was somewhat different with life tenants, at least from the time of Richard the Second. A statute passed in that reign,‡ which had the most important conse-

---

* Bacon, Treatise on the Use of the Law.   † Ibid.   ‡ St. 9 Ric. II., c. 3.

quences on the future history of settlements, furnished the heir with means of avoiding any adverse judgment obtained by the collusion or default of a life tenant in possession; but no such remedy was ever granted to the heir of an entail, if we except the protection afforded him by the process of *formedon*,[*] which, as soon as it was really tested, immediately proved fallacious. The method pursued in Taltarum's case was really extremely simple, and the complicated system of common recoveries—the legal drama in which the demandant, the tenant to the *præcipe*, the tenant in tail, and the common vouchee, each played a *rôle* elaborately rehearsed —was of later growth. In the former case, the tenant in possession simply vouched a "dummy" lord, supposed to be the representative of the original grantor, to warrant his title; the dummy duly made default; and judgment was pronounced for the plaintiff, the tenant in tail in remainder being supposed to have a remedy, which of course was barred by the attendant circumstances, against the defaulting warrantor.[†] Such in brief was the process by which entailed estates once more recovered their plasticity; and as Parliament, which had refused to confer, did not interfere to destroy the privilege, we must suppose, to adopt the phrase of the modern jurist, that the wisdom of the legislature commanded what it tacitly allowed. Such proceedings of course in time became far from uncommon; and at length they may be said to have received indirect parliamentary sanction from a series of enactments which in the sequel opened up another method of effecting the same result.

The assurances which went by the name of *fines*—so called because they were said to put an end to the disputes of the various claimants to an estate—were not originally capable of being applied to estates tail. The power of barring future claims by this means was taken away by a statute of Edward III.,[‡] but restored with some extensions as to time, and the further condition of proclamation in open court, by enactments of Richard III. and Henry VII.;[§] and

---

[*] 3 Blackst. Comm., 191-193.   [†] Williams, Real Property, pp. 43, 44.
[‡] St. 34 Edw. III. c. 13.   [§] St. 1 Ric. III. c. 7 : 4 Hen. VII. c. 24.

by a judicial construction of the latter act* a fine levied by a tenant in tail was for the first time allowed to bar the title of his issue, in the event of no claim being made by them within the following five years. In the next reign, a further act was passed, which rendered a bar so effected immediate ;† and the only difference between a fine and a common recovery from that date consisted in the circumstance that by the former only the issue, by the latter all remainders and reversionary interests as well, could be effectually barred; a circumstance which seems to prove conclusively that the feeling of the legislature in the reign of Henry the Eighth was distinctly hostile to any pretensions to an indefeasible right of succession on the part of the eldest son. The power of a tenant in tail in possession to alienate during life was thus firmly established, and has not since been questioned. The method however of effecting this object was long felt to be unnecessarily complicated; and at length, in the last reign, on the recommendation of the Real Property Commissioners, fines and recoveries were entirely abolished, and a simple deed, executed by the tenant and enrolled in the Court of Chancery, substituted in their place.‡

It was also in the reign of Henry VIII. that, by the Statute of Wills, a free power of testamentary disposition was once more conceded; with regard to lands held by knight's service, it was, however, as has been already mentioned, restricted to two-thirds of the estate; but since there was no such limitation on conveyance *inter vivos*, this provision cannot have been very severely felt; and when, on the Restoration, all tenures in the kingdom were converted into free and common socage,§ the liberty of bequest became universally complete.

It is important to observe that in the middle ages, from the time when collusive recoveries and fines were first applied to entailed estates, down to the period when the system of contingent remainders was elaborated, and the

* Williams, Real Property. p. 48 nt. c.
† The account of these enactments is based on Williams, R. P., pp. 47, 48.
‡ St. 3 and 4 Will. IV. c. 74.   § St. 12 Car. II. c. 24.

practice of making family settlements arose, the power over landed property entrusted to the tenant in possession was greater than he has enjoyed either before or since. That this liberty was on the whole beneficial to the country, at the time when it was exercised, can scarcely be a matter of doubt; although this admission does not necessarily involve the unqualified condemnation of the more restrictive system which has arisen under the changed economical and social conditions of modern times. It would moreover be extremely rash to conclude that the right of disinheriting was frequently resorted to, or that the privilege of the eldest son, which custom so long had sanctioned, at once or in many cases fell into desuetude. " Younger brothers are commonly fortunate," writes Bacon, in his essay on Parents and Children, "but seldom or never, where the elder are disinherited;" and the numerous instances in which to our knowledge large landed estates were transmitted practically intact through all the vicissitudes of the Tudor and the Stuart reigns lead us to believe that at the time when Primogeniture was in the strictest sense a custom, and a custom which borrowed little support from law, it was scarcely less generally and strenuously maintained than under the Plantagenet or the Hanoverian line.

Family pride and legal ingenuity were busily engaged under the Stuarts in the effort to reimpose on landed property the fetters from which it had escaped, and their endeavours were ultimately rewarded with complete success. The celebrated decision in Shelley's case, pronounced in the time of Coke, must have frustrated many efforts to prevent alienation by deciding that to give a tenant for life a remainder in fee-simple or in tail was merely to "limit" the estate—that is, if legal phraseology be converted into plain English, to render the possessor's power as unlimited as possible. But other and more effectual methods of attaining the desired object were soon devised. By the statute of Richard II.* above referred to a tenant for life only, in possession, could not suffer a recovery without its being

* St. 9 Ric. II. c. 3.

liable to be set aside at the instance of the heir; while if he held the land, by conveyance or settlement, to himself and his heirs, or himself and the heirs of his body, the expectation of the latter could at any time be defeated. Accordingly, the heir was now described in deeds not as such but as the *eldest son*; and in the construction of such instruments the judges held that the son, when he came into existence, took by the donor's gift and did not inherit from his father.

Contingent remainders of this kind however were soon found to be not perfectly secure. A contingent remainder may be briefly described as an estate *not* ready, like a vested remainder, to come into possession at any moment after its limitation when the prior estate may happen to determine. It is an estate future not merely in possession but also in interest. It being then an ancient maxim of feudal law that the seisin must never be left without an owner, if the contingent remainder did not *vest* during the continuance of the preceding particular estate, that is, if the future interest in question did not become a present one before the expiration, or on the instant of the expiration, of that which went before it, the remainder was entirely void. In consequence of this principle, means were discovered by life tenants of voiding contingent remainders. The tenant for life surrendered his estate, or conveyed it away, or procured its merger by purchasing a vested remainder in fee-simple; and if he adopted any of these courses before the birth of a son, the future interest of the latter was entirely destroyed. It was in order to defeat these proceedings that some of the leading lawyers of the Restoration invented the system of appointing *trustees* to preserve contingent remainders, who, by the terms of the deed in each case, were to come into possession in the event of the particular estate determining otherwise than by the decease of the life tenant, in order to support the remainder and give it an opportunity of vesting before his death. The invention of this plan is generally ascribed to Sir Orlando Bridgman,* who, it will be re-

* 2 Blackst. Comm. 172. Neate, History, &c. p. 14. The latter rather strongly observes:—" It was then only that the Law of Entail was effectually

membered, held the Great Seal as Keeper in 1672, before the Chancellorship of Shaftesbury. It continued to be in use until the present reign, when the enactment of a statute to preserve contingent remainders, notwithstanding the forfeiture, surrender or merger of the particular estate, rendered the appointment of trustees no longer necessary.* The only restraint which the wisdom of the law has imposed on the creation of these estates is that they cannot be limited to an *unborn* person with remainder to his children, the remainder in such cases being absolutely void.† The law considers that it thus vindicates the assertion that it "abhors perpetuities;" and the substantial effect of the rule is that property can be tied up for a life, or any number of lives, in being, and for twenty-one years afterwards. A tenant in tail in possession can always bar the entail; and if his estate is in remainder he can equally do so, with the consent of the "Protector" of the settlement, who is nearly always the life tenant in possession.‡

We are now in a position to consider the operation of the ordinary settlement of modern times, and to appreciate the absurdity of the vulgar belief that much of the property in this country is "heir land," that is, that it is so bound to a certain course of devolution that no individual owner can ever modify its descent.§ In point of fact, property which is constantly kept in the same family is so confined by the custom of Primogeniture, which dictates the character of periodical re-settlements, occurring on an average once in

restored, and that mosaic of legal antiquities—that thing of shreds and patches of dead law, or rather of fraudulent evasions of legal principle and legislative enactment—which is called a Marriage Settlement, received its full completion."

* St. 8 & 9 Vict. c. 106.

† The only exception to this rule lies in the application by the courts of the *cy près* doctrine, when such dispositions are effected by *will*. In such cases the unborn son acquires not a mere *life* estate—as he would if the grant had been made by deed—but an estate tail, so that his own children have a *possibility* of inheriting.

‡ St. 3 & 4 Will. IV. c. 74.

§ There are of course some few properties—such as Blenheim and Strathfieldsaye—held directly of the State, which are altogether inalienable, except by consent of the legislature; but these depend on the special enactment which created them.

each generation. The usual course is for the son, who is tenant in tail in remainder, on marrying, or sometimes immediately on attaining his majority, to concur with his father, the protector of the settlement, in re-settling the estate. The entail is barred; the son becomes tenant for life in remainder expectant on his father's death; and a contingent remainder in tail is limited to his unborn heir. Advantage is taken of the re-settlement to provide for the liquidation of outstanding liabilities, and to ensure, by means either of rent-charges or powers, what may be considered a suitable provision by way of jointure for the widow, and annuities for the younger sons. If the re-settlement is effected on the son's marriage, these objects are in themselves ordinarily sufficient to induce him to assent to it; if at a period before he contemplates marriage, he is usually compensated for the sacrifice to which he submits, in exchanging a tenancy in tail for a life interest, by an addition to his allowance, granted out of the estate, sufficient to enable him to keep up his position with dignity and comfort, or by such other means as family affection or convenience may suggest. But if the son should chance to be insensible to any of these considerations—a very rare contingency—there is no means whatever of compelling him to surrender his vested expectancy in tail, which he can exchange, the moment he acquires possession, for a fee-simple estate.

Before proceeding to consider the economical and other objections which have been urged against this system, it may be worth while to give a brief account of the history of entails in Scotland, which presents some features different from those with which we are familiar in other parts of the kingdom.

The modern system of entailing appears to have arisen in Scotland at about the same time as that at which the device of contingent remainders was perfected in England by the lawyers of the Restoration. It is stated that the first recorded instance of an entail occurred on the Roxburgh property in 1648; but as this and other instruments copied from its example were made at common law, and were without statutory sanction, it was considered doubtful whether an action to set them aside might not prove successful.* Such an attempt was made in 1662 in the Court of Session, but the Court, by a small majority, sustained the entail. The point however was not considered to have been definitely decided by this judgment; it was notorious that the "factors" which influenced the opinions of members of that Court were somewhat complicated; able lawyers were understood to have expressed an opinion that the judgment was founded on policy rather than law;† and entails were still regarded with little confidence until in 1685 an enactment—entitled "an Act concerning tallies"—was passed,‡ which fully established the legality of the practice, and permitted the creation of entails of a perpetual character§ which have never been allowed or tolerated by the law of England. On the other hand, the same statute established the principle of compulsory public registration of all entails, and of all deeds and provisions relating thereto, a principle which has since then been invariably maintained in Scotland, with results which, so to speak, have accentuated the grievance of Englishmen, and made them more keenly sensible of the disadvantage under which they labour through

---

* McCulloch, Treatise on Succession, p. 52.

† "The courts of law in Scotland have seldom, even in modern times, been satisfied with endeavouring to administer the existing law fairly and impartially; but have usually endeavoured to make their decisions square with their own views of what is right and proper."—McCulloch, p. 67, note. Mr. McCulloch goes on to say that in later times the feeling of the courts was very hostile to the system of perpetual entails, and that they accordingly refused to restrain practices which were obviously most injurious not only to the expectant heir but to the public as well. "The House of Lords, however, pronounced such practices to be illegal; and conveyed to the Court of Sessions a very distinct intimation that it was their duty fairly to administer the law as it stood, and to leave its alteration and amendment to the legislature."—Ibid.

‡ St. 1 Jac. vii., c. 22.

§ By this Act, "all his Majesty's subjects are empowered to tallie their lands and estates in Scotland with such provisions and conditions as they shall think fit, and with such irritant and resolutive clauses as to them shall seem proper." Mr. McCulloch says of the Act :—"It reduced heirs of entail to the condition (nearly) of tenants for life, and gave entailers power to regulate the perpetual destination of their property, subject only to the obligation of enrolling the entail, with its various clauses and provisions, in a public register, there to remain (such are the words of the act) *ad perpetuam rei memoriam.*"—P. 53.

the absence from this country of any general system of the same kind.

The secure establishment of the privileges of the eldest son appears to have been only a secondary object of the enactment of James II. The primary object of the Estates was apparently the protection of landed property, by means of entails, from those forfeitures which were then so frightfully frequent, and which exposed the estate of even the most loyal and well-affected owner to confiscation whenever the caprice, the rancour or the suspicions of the Crown, the cupidity and avarice of courtiers, the supple ingenuity of the lawyers, and the cringing servility of the judges, combined to institute a fresh prosecution and condemn another victim. As soon, in fact, as the Stuart dynasty was expelled, an Act was passed which expressly exempted entailed property from forfeiture; but on the union of the two kingdoms the Scotch law of treason was assimilated to that of England, and from that time forward up to the enactment in 1870 of the statute* by which all attainders are now abolished, the rule in both countries was that the attainder of a tenant in tail forfeited the estate to his heirs, though without prejudice to the interests of remainder men.

The forfeitures of Scotch estates under the then existing law, which resulted from the rebellions of 1715 and 1745, were extremely numerous, and much public attention was directed to the matter. It was this controversy which produced Mr. Charles Yorke's well-known pamphlet, "Considerations on the Law of Forfeiture for High Treasons," Mr. Yorke arguing, much as it was contended by the opponents of strict entails and the exemption from forfeiture which they then implied, after the passing of *De Donis*, that the liability to such a consequence was an additional security for the good behaviour and loyalty of the tenant in possession.† Such reasoning seems to have been at the time

* St. 33 & 34 Vict. c. 23.

† Mr. McCulloch speaks of Mr. Yorke's treatise as being practically a commentary on the theory of Cicero: *Nec vero me fugit quam sic acerbum parentum scelera filiorum pœnis lui; sed hoc prœclare legibus comparatum est ut caritas liberorum amiciores parentes rei publicœ redderet.*---Ep. ad Brutum.

considered adequate; and there was no subsequent occasion on which any grievance on a large scale was experienced from the operation of the law.

The statute of 1685 had established a system of perpetual entails; and until less than thirty years ago the law of Scotland continued on nearly the same footing. During one hundred and sixty years from the "Act Concerning Tallies" Scotch law maintained entails as rigorously as English law had done during the period, nearly the same in length, which followed the enactment of *De donis*. The Courts however were hostile to the principle, and did their best to obviate some of its natural consequences; but these efforts were on the whole ill-directed; and attempts to evade the law by the introduction of an illegal elasticity were liable to defeat, and were frequently defeated, by an appeal to the House of Lords. Up to the year 1770, an entailer might prohibit as well the granting of leases as the charging of the estate with any debts. It was very generally felt that such conditions were so hostile to improvement as to require legislative interference; and accordingly in that year an Act was passed "for the Improvement of Lands, &c., held in Scotland under settlements of strict entail."[*] The provisions of this statute, commonly known as the Montgomery Act, will be noticed in detail in the following section.[†] Six years before it was passed, considerable endeavours had been made in Scotland to altogether abolish the system of perpetual entails. The Faculty of Advocates were nearly unanimous in their dislike to such a system of tenure; and a bill was drawn up, on the suggestion of Lord Kames, which would have practically assimilated the Scotch system to that of England. The project, however, after considerable discussion eventually fell through; and matters continued on the footing on which they had been placed by the "Act concerning Tallies" until 1848.

It was an inevitable consequence of this condition of the law that the proportion of strictly entailed property in Scotland to that free from such restrictions should be con-

---

[*] St. 10 Geo. III. c. 51.   [†] See p. 106, *infra*.

stantly on the increase. Adam Smith, writing towards the close of the last century, considered that more than one-fifth, and perhaps one-third, of the land in Scotland was then under strict entail. The practice has since that period been continued with great rapidity. We learn from the public register that during the twenty years between 1685 and 1705, 79 entails were recorded; during the next twenty years the number amounted to 125; and it steadily increased, with a progression exceeding that of arithmetrical ratio, until in the corresponding period of the end of the last and beginning of the present century the number of such deeds reached 360; while the total during the twenty years immediately following—from 1805 to 1825—was no less than 459. Making due allowance for the circumstance that a considerable number of the deeds so recorded were not really new entails, but referred to those which had been set aside or terminated, or were themselves merely instruments of revocation or explanation, there is still every reason to believe that Mr. McCulloch who, writing in 1847,[*] estimated the quantity of entailed land in Scotland as exceeding one-half of the whole, was certainly not guilty of exaggeration.[†]

At length, in 1848, the attention of Parliament was directed—partly perhaps by Mr. McCulloch's treatise—to the constant and dangerously rapid growth of this practice; and by an Act passed in that year [‡] a tenant in tail in possession, if born after 1848, and of full age, may cut off the entail without the consent of the next "heir substitute" being

---

[*] Mr. Brodrick is in error in stating (Cobden Club Essays, Second Series, p. 67) that Mr. McCulloch wrote in 1849, after the passing of the statute of 1848 for facilitating disentailing. Mr. McCulloch's treatise, which was based on an article by the same writer in the *Edinburgh Review* for July, 1824, was re-written and completed, as appears from the Preface, not later than December, 1847, and was published in 1848. It therefore naturally makes no reference to the Act of that year, a knowledge of which Mr. Brodrick incorrectly attributes to the author.

[†] p. 57. According to the General Report of Scotland published in 1814 the valued rent of land in that country amounted in 1811 to £3,804,221, while that of entailed estates amounted to £1,213,279, or nearly a third of the whole.

[‡] St. 11 & 12 Vict. c. 36 : see also 16 & 17 Vict c. 94.

required. Moreover, if he is himself the only heir in existence, and if he is of full age, and unmarried, he requires no person's consent; while in other cases the consent of all the next heirs substitute, if less than three in number, is necessary, or, if they are three or more, of the next three heirs; and in the latter case it is further required that the first of the three—the heir apparent or "next heir substitute"—shall be himself no less than *twenty-five* years of age, and free from any disability.

In consequence of this Act, the position of a Scotch tenant in tail has been evidently assimilated to a great extent, though by no means completely, to the comparative liberty enjoyed by his English counterpart. In point of fact, however, the occupier in Scotland of land under entail still labours, it is held, under considerable grievances, particularly as to his security for agricultural improvements, which have been to a great extent removed in England; and the matter has within the present month* been brought under the notice of Lord Hartington, who, speaking with the caution befitting one who is not only a distinguished statesman *in esse*, but a great landed proprietor *in futuro*, has promised it his most attentive consideration. We are now, however, after sketching the history of the Scotch system, which may be said to view perpetuities with no disfavour, in a better position to consider the merits of those objections which from an economical point of view have been urged against the English law, which on the whole may fairly claim to "abhor" them; while, before proceeding in another section to this important portion of our subject, it is certainly instructive to observe that, despite all that has been said of the insuperable obstacles to agricultural improvement involved in a system of perpetual entails—statements which doubtless contain a very great amount of truth—the development of agricultural enterprise and the progress of advanced methods of cultivation in Scotland, during the last century, has been at least as steady and at least as rapid as in any other European country; and this statement, the truth of

* November, 1877.

which no competent inquirer would ever question, is by no means to be confined in its application to those estates which various circumstances have hitherto preserved from the influence of entails.*

* In an Appendix to the Sketches of the History of Man, published in 1774, Lord Kames says, "The quantity of land that is locked up in Scotland by entails has damped the growing spirit of agriculture. There is not produced sufficiency of corn at home for our consumption, and our condition will become worse and worse by new entails, till agriculture and industry be annihilated." Now, the extent of land under entail in Scotland has been certainly more than doubled, perhaps more than trebled, since this paragraph was written; and yet agriculture and manufactures have made a more rapid progress in the interval, and especially during the last thirty years, when entails were most prevalent, than in England, or in any other country whatever.—McCulloch, p. 71.

SECTION IV.—ECONOMICAL ASPECTS OF PRIMOGENITURE.

THE ultimate right of the State to determine by legislative enactment the conditions under which property in land shall be acquired, enjoyed and transmitted by its subjects has seldom if ever been questioned either by philosophers or politicians, or by the landowners themselves. It was asserted on many occasions by the various states of Greece and the republic of Rome; and if it was not habitually exercised by the nominal sovereign or chief in those more primitive forms of social life out of which the polity both of Greece and Rome arose, and of which more than one type has survived until nearly the present age, the reason lay in the fact that the Village Community—which claimed the right of portioning its land among its members as seemed most expedient—was itself in all matters of fiscal policy and economical organisation the real and sole sovereign.* It is indeed an easy task to adduce substantial reasons in support of that axiom of Montesquieu, which stands at the head of this essay, and to justify the State in regulating the tenure of landed property to an extent which if applied to other forms of wealth would assuredly prove most injurious. The land, as has been poetically remarked, is "the leaf on which we live;" it is the ultimate source of all production and consequently of all wealth. The ownership or possession of land moreover has in many countries and in many ages constituted the sole claim to political rights, a circumstance in itself sufficient, *wherever it exists*, to justify a demand that such ownership should be easily accessible to every citizen. Again land, unlike almost every other form of riches, is strictly limited in amount; and any condition of the law which tends to restrict the chance of acquiring a thing, in

---

* I may illustrate my meaning by referring to Sir Henry Maine's interesting criticism of some of Austin's theories in the "Early History of Institutions" (Lecture XIII. *Sovereignty and Empire*) and especially to his remarks on the so-called sovereignty exercised by the Sikh chieftains in the Punjaub (pp. 380-382) and by the Assyrian and Babylonian Empires, many centuries before, over their remote dependencies (pp. 384, 385).

itself desirable and limited in quantity, to a small fraction of the entire population, may perhaps be regarded as *prima facie* objectionable, if not unjust. As a matter of fact, the majority of European countries have from time to time passed laws intended to prevent the accumulation of extremely large quantities of land in the hands of comparatively few proprietors; and the measures, from an economical point of view most pernicious, recently passed by one of our Australian colonies,* imposing a property tax on a scale graduated according to wealth, must indirectly operate in the same direction. Laws regulating the method of cultivation have at various times been still more numerous, and have indeed been frequently of imperative necessity. It cannot however be too strongly urged that the less we have to do with such laws the better. The more a State finds itself able to trust to the public spirit, intelligence and enterprise of its individual members, and the more, in consequence of the existence of such characteristics, it feels able to leave them at liberty to administer and dispose of their property without external interference, the healthier, we may be assured, will be the general condition of such a State, and the more certain and rapid its progress in industrial and agricultural improvement. The more an individual is left to himself, the more he will be likely to exert himself; if invested with plenary legal rights, the chance is far greater that he will not be unmindful of the correlative

---

* A careful summary of the present aspect of the Land Tax question in Victoria will be found in the *Times*, Nov. 23, 1877. It appears that the bill, enthusiastically supported by the people, has been accepted with extreme reluctance by the Legislative Council, and only in order to avoid a direct collision with the Ministry and the Lower House. By its provisions, all estates of less than £5000 in value are exempted from taxation, but when that limit is passed a duty is imposed of 25s. per cent. on the capital value of the land. It is anticipated that the tax will affect less than a thousand proprietors, but that it will produce £200,000 a year, or one-tenth of the "taxation proper" of the colony. It is stated that "the Bill was primarily designed to prevent the formation of extensive landed estates in the hands of individual proprietors, and to compel those who now hold large estates to break up their holdings." Mr. Lowe's remarks, in his article on "A New Reform Bill" (*Fortnightly Review*, Oct. 1877) on the connection between democracy and the *impôt progressif* theory, as illustrated by the proposed legislation in Victoria, are worth comparing.

moral duties which his position involves; and there can be little doubt that one of the surest incentives to enterprise lies in the consciousness that the man who has made the most of his opportunities is free not only himself to enjoy the benefit of the wealth he has accumulated but to dispose of it, on his decease, at his absolute discretion. It cannot be said that legislative interference with the rights of individual owners is in all cases unjustifiable; but we may at least contend that it always requires justification. Other circumstances may occur of such paramount importance as to override the considerations adduced above; but the existence of such circumstances must be abundantly demonstrated, ere a case for the curtailment of the "rights of property" can be adequately made out.

The States of ancient Greece appear to have in many cases followed a policy in one respect in harmony, in another entirely inconsistent, with the views of many modern economists. They objected to any of their citizens acquiring property in land to an extent greatly in excess of that enjoyed by their fellows; and an equalisation of lots was a favourite scheme of legislators and philosophers. On the other hand, they did not regard with favour the extension of facilities for the transfer of landed property, and endeavoured as much as possible to retain in the occupation of the descendants the soil which the ancestors had tilled. The absence of such efforts at Sparta, and the consequent concentration of wealth in the hands of a constantly diminishing number, was pointed out by Aristotle as one of the gravest defects in the constitution of that state.* Such a social condition could not indeed fail to produce disastrous consequences under a system like that of Sparta, where citizenship entirely depended on a property qualification, and where the only form of property which an exclusively military and agricultural people, who considered all industry as servile and degrading, could possibly possess

---

* μετὰ γὰρ τὰ νῦν ῥηθέντα τοῖς περὶ τὴν ἀνωμαλίαν τῆς κτήσεως ἐπιτιμήσειεν ἄν τις· τοῖς μὲν γὰρ αὐτῶν συμβέβηκε κεκτῆσθαι πολλὴν λίαν οὐσίαν, τοῖς δὲ πάμπαν μικράν· διόπερ εἰς ὀλίγους ἥκει ἡ χώρα.—Ar. Pol. ii. 9.

consisted of proprietary rights in the soil. Laws, moreover, encouraging population by giving special exemptions from public service to the fathers of numerous families directly contributed to increase the pressure of the people on the land at a time when there were no facilities for emigrating or for colonization on a large scale. It may now be considered as proved, by Mr. Grote's most exhaustive argument, that the supposed Lycurgean partition of the soil, so long assumed on the authority of Plutarch, had no existence in fact; that inequality of distribution had always been more or less characteristic of the tenure of property in Sparta; and that under the peculiar conditions of that State it in the end produced disastrous consequences, of which the most serious was a steady diminution in the number of properly qualified citizens. The circumstance that Aristotle mentions Phaleas of Chalcedon* as the earliest author of an agrarian law of which the object was the equalisation of property furnishes another indirect argument against any such legislation having been attempted by Lycurgus. The difficulty of course lay in maintaining such equality as a permanent condition; and some, the philosopher tells us, attempted to do so by regulating the number of children, others by limiting the indefinite extension of individual property, others by forbidding the sale of inherited estates. In point of fact, in order to preserve in its original strictness the main features of the scheme of Phaleas it would probably have been necessary to resort to all these measures; and the only other method of carrying out his intention would have been to introduce a law of primogeniture—which, it is rather curious to observe, seems never to have suggested itself to the legislators of ancient Greece†—accompanied by a system of strict perpetuities forbidding alienation under any circumstances. Such a law, in a land where other forms of wealth were unknown, would have gone far, especially if accompanied by restrictions on over-population, to preserve the original lots

* Ar. Pol. II. 7.
† The trifling privileges spoken of by Demosthenes in the speech for Phormio, above referred to, as πρεσβεῖα, and others mentioned in the same place, are scarcely sufficient to qualify this statement.

according to the distribution of the legislator; but it would have inevitably brought innumerable difficulties and grievances in its train; and entirely as the Greek citizen was considered to live not for himself but for the state, completely as the good of the individual was subordinated to the common weal, such violent interference with the rights and liberties of the members of the community appears to have been always regarded as practically out of the question. Plato, in his *Laws*, recognises the existence of a certain amount of inequality as inevitable, but proposes that no citizen should be allowed to own more than five times as much property as his fellows. In another part of his political treatise, Aristotle mentions other schemes which had come under his knowledge and observation. That form of popular government which he viewed with most favour —the " agricultural democracy "—required, he thought, as a condition of stability that no one should be allowed to hold more than a certain quantity of land. A law of Oxylus, an Elean legislator, which forbade the citizen to encumber more than a prescribed proportion of his land with mortgage debts appears to have powerfully aided in perpetuating ancestral estates in the same family;[*] while the Aphytean lawgiver, by assessing taxation on a small portion only of the property of each citizen, enabled all to satisfy the qualification for political privileges.[†] The foregoing illustrations shew that the general policy of the Greek legislator, while opposed to large estates, was equally unfavourable to alienation; and this principle, in its origin partly to be explained by that connection between the family land and the family religion which has been adverted to above, owed its justification, at a later period, to the intimate relation which in Greece subsisted between political and proprietary rights.

At Rome, the ancient equivalent of representation—the right of exercising the suffrage of a burgess in the as-

[*] Ar. Pol. VII. (Vulg. VI.) 4.

[†] *Ibid.* τιμῶνται γὰρ οὐκ ὅλας τὰς κτήσεις, ἀλλὰ κατὰ τηλικαῦτα μόρια διαιροῦντες ὥστ' ἔχειν ὑπερβάλλειν ταῖς τιμήσεσι καὶ τοὺς πένητας.

semblies of the people—depended, if not on taxation, at least on that liability to contribute to state purposes which enrolment on the census implied; and the famous Agrarian Laws of the republic were doubtless closely connected with this object. It has sometimes been stated that their purpose was to restrict the amount of land tenable by a single owner; but it may well be doubted whether they ever so far interfered with individual rights, and were not rather confined to regulating the conditions on which the Patricians might occupy or *possess* the *public* or domainial land. Their main intention was doubtless to encourage and protect the agricultural class which was justly recognised as the sinews of the state; the reasons for their ultimate failure have been admirably elucidated by Dr. Mommson;[*] and one of the principal causes doubtless lay in the circumstance that no legislation succeeded in effectually checking the accumulation of enormous estates, worked exclusively by slaves, in the hands of a few proprietors. The existence of such estates, coupled with the injudicious system of importing corn and freely distributing it among the ever more numerous mob of the metropolis—the *fruges consumere nati*—who gradually superseded the whole class of burgesses and obtained the exclusive control of the comitia, in the end caused the class of small farmers completely to disappear and, as Pliny tells us, ruined the agricultural system first of Italy and ultimately of the provinces as well.[†]

The enactments of almost all European states have been in modern times distinctly unfavourable to the existence of large estates, and in many of the countries which have borrowed the principles of the *Code Napoléon* as their guide in regulating the tenure of landed property it has become practically impossible to maintain them undivided for any length of time. In England, on the contrary, they have been allowed and even favourably regarded by the

[*] History of Rome; See especially Vol. II. Book III. c. 12 : "The management of land and of capital" (pp. 385-418) and Vol. III. Bk. IV. c 11 : "The commonwealth and its economy" (esp. pp. 427, 428).

[†] *Latifundia* perdidere Italiam, iam vero et provincias. Nat. Hist. xviii. 6, 35.

law ; the lawyers have seconded with their highest skill and ingenuity the efforts of landowners to perpetuate them in the hands of their descendants ; and the principles on which *intestate* succession to real property is determined have exercised a certain direct influence by their operation and produced a still greater indirect effect by the example they supply. Many writers have in recent times advocated the adoption in our own country of some system having for its object that equalization of property which the legislators of Greece and Rome with more or less earnestness, but invariably with small success, endeavoured to establish, and which the succession laws of modern times have in other lands in great measure succeeded in effecting. The right of the State to control, direct, or modify the method in which land is owned and occupied by its subjects has already been shewn to be one which may be legitimately asserted. I have also endeavoured to shew that it is one of those latent rights of which only extreme and urgent necessity justifies the exercise ; and it remains to inquire whether the present conditions of tenure in England are such as imperatively to demand the interference of the legislature, or whether they are not on the contrary of such a character that any amelioration which might be thus effected would be more than counterbalanced by the pernicious feeling of insecurity which such interposition must inevitably create.

It has not hitherto been an easy task to discover the precise number of landed proprietors in England; but it is generally admitted to be small in comparison with the number occupying a similar extent of soil in other European countries ; while if we contrast the state of affairs in our own country with that prevailing among our immediate neighbours across the Channel the difference is certainly of a most striking kind. In France the principle of subdivision has probably been carried to a further extent than in any other country: in England, " the Herculaneum," as it has been called, " of Feudalism," the opposite principle still maintains its influence undiminished. Mr. McCulloch, writing thirty years ago, shewed that there were good grounds for inferring from various statistics which he quotes that the number of proprietors of land in France was at that time between four millions and four millions and a half; from which it appeared that since the whole population, including women and children, amounted in 1846 to rather more than thirty-five millions, nearly two-thirds of the entire number fell under the category of landed proprietors.* Mr. Cliffe Leslie, writing only seven years ago,† mentions that the latest French official statistics reckoned nearly *eight million* proprietors, of whom, according to a calculation of M. de Lavergne, not less than five millions were rural proprietors, and nearly four millions small proprietors who cultivated their land themselves without hired labour.‡ Three million French proprietors, according to M. Lavergne,§ possessed on the average only a single hectare—less than two acres and a half—apiece, while the average extent of the properties of the remaining two millions did not exceed six hectares, or about fourteen acres each. ||

When we turn to England, the picture which presents itself is certainly of a very different kind. Until more accurate information was quite recently procured, it used to be frequently stated that there were in England only 30,000 landowners. This assertion, which rests on the circumstance that in the Occupation Returns of the last census but one only 30,766 persons described themselves as "landed proprietors," is in itself so palpably absurd as scarcely to require refutation. A sufficient disproof of its correctness may however be gathered from the circumstance that above half of these thirty thousand persons belonged to the feminine sex; a fact which an ingenious writer has explained by the sug-

* That is, estimating the families at an average of five persons each—perhaps rather too high an average for France.

† Systems of Land Tenure in Various Countries, pp. 336, 337.

‡ The exact number of those cultivating the land *de leur mains* was, according to the official returns of 1851, 3,740,793. It must have considerably increased since that date.

§ Economie Rurale de la France.

|| Similarly in Prussia, with a population of about 24,000,000 the number of proprietors—including apparently urban with rural, which I have not done in the case of France—was estimated in 1871 at no less than five millions.

gestion that women owning land feel a pride " in recording their ownership; whereas thousands of male landowners returned themselves as peers, members of Parliament, bankers, merchants or private gentlemen. At all events," he justly continues, " the mere existence of so palpable a flaw in the return utterly destroys its value for the purposes of statistical argument."* Particular instructions to obtain precise information on this matter were issued to the officers charged with superintending the census returns of 1871; but better and more trustworthy statistics than could possibly be obtained by means of the census are embodied in a Parliamentary return, enumerating the proprietors of land in England and Wales, together with the amount owned by each proprietor, which was moved for by Lord Derby in February, 1872. Lord Derby dwelt upon the outcry frequently raised against the monopoly of land, and added that he believed it to have been in part produced by the erroneous impression to which the census of 1861 gave rise.† He himself considered that the number of landed proprietors in the United Kingdom was nearer to 300,000 than 30,000. Mr. Brodrick, writing in the previous year, had come to the conclusion that the number in England and Wales alone greatly exceeded 100,000, and might well amount to 200,000. The motion, which was supported by the Duke of Richmond and Lord Salisbury, was acceded to, on the part of the government, by Lord Halifax, and the return was duly prepared by the Local Government Board, on the basis of the valuation lists made out for the purposes of rating in every parish. The result, after considerable delay, inevitable owing to the incompleteness of the information in many cases procurable and the thoroughness with which the work was done, was published in 1875, and substantially confirmed the conjecture of Lord Derby. " The New Domesday Book," as it has been popularly called, elicited to a great extent that public attention and interest

* Brodrick, Hon. G. C., Cobden Club Essays, second series, p. 74.

† Thus, according to the census of 1861, the number of proprietors in Hertfordshire was only 245. The Marquis of Salisbury determined to test this surprising statement for himself, and found that according to the rate-book the number at the time amounted to 8833 !

which its intrinsic importance deserved. The names of owners were divided into those who held at least one acre, and those who held portions of land—frequently occupied for building purposes—of less extent; and it appeared that the number of proprietors falling under the first of these two categories, in England and Wales alone, amounted to 269,547. This statement however must be regarded as only approximately correct. In the first place the metropolitan district was expressly excluded from the return; secondly, it is to be observed that holders of leases for a period *exceeding* 99 years, or with a *right* of perpetual renewal, were considered as owners, although their interest in the land, in the eye of the law, is of a merely personal kind. Lastly, in cases where an owner held property in more than one county, it was an inevitable consequence of the method by which the statistics were procured that his name should appear twice over; and it is estimated from an examination of a certain proportion of names that a deduction of about 6000 from the total given should for this reason be effected in order to arrive at the net number of proprietors of one acre or more of land. On the whole it may fairly be assumed, as a result of this return, that there are in England and Wales at the present time as nearly as possible 250,000 proprietors of freehold estates not less than one acre in extent.

The entire number of owners of less than an acre of land—many of them doubtless merely tenants for terms, and none of them with any claim to be practically considered as rural proprietors—was slightly over 700,000. The return unfortunately does not contain any tabular statement of the proportion of acreage and rental held by these two classes respectively. A glance at the returns for the individual counties is however sufficient to shew that while the gross *rental* of the second class is considerable—often amounting to a half or a third and perhaps averaging a quarter of that enjoyed by the first class—the *acreage* which it holds is altogether insignificant; a circumstance which contributes to prove that land held in quantities of less than an acre in the main is held for building or industrial rather than for agricultural purposes.*

Leaving then out of the question, as not really belonging to the category of rural proprietors, the owners of land less than an acre in extent, we find that the proprietary class in England, so far from being reckoned by millions as in France and Prussia, is composed of about a quarter of a million persons. The industry of statisticians however has placed us in a position to estimate with greater exactitude than these figures of themselves could furnish the proportion of land held by really large proprietors to the total acreage of the country. It appears from a computation made by a writer in the *Spectator*† that the number of owners of freehold property in England and Wales exceeding *one hundred acres* in extent is only 42,469; a figure which goes far to explain the readiness with which the erroneous computation contained in the census of 1861 was generally accepted as correct. We learn, moreover, from a later article in the same journal, that no more than 710 individuals owned between them "within a fraction of a fourth of the entire geographical area of England and Wales," and enjoyed, either immediately or in reversion, about one-seventh of the entire rental of the kingdom, a proportion which would, it is thought, have been consider-

---

* Thus in Bedfordshire, Class A (in number 2382) held 285,000 acres with a gross estimated rental exceeding £580,000, or rather more than £2 per acre. Class B (in no. 5302) held only 824 acres, but with a rental of £134,000 or more than £160 an acre. In Devon, Class A (10,162) held 1,500,000 acres at an average rental of as exactly as possible £1 10s. per acre; while Class B (21,647) held 3000 acres at an average rental of £200 per acre. In Gloucester, Class A (8425) held 720,000 acres at an average rental of rather more than £2 an acre; while Class B (29,280) held 6000 acres at an average rental of about £160 per acre (the result being the same with both classes as in Bedfordshire). In Hereford, Class A (4646) held 500,000 acres at an average rental of rather more than £1 10s.; Class B (9085) held 1300 acres at an average rental of £88 per acre; lastly, in Lancashire Class A (12,558) held 930,000 acres at an average rental of nearly £8 per acre : Class B (76,177) held 15,000 acres at an average rental of about £430 per acre. It is remarkable that in Kent, notwithstanding the operation of the rule of gavelkind, the proportion, in number of proprietors, extent and value of acreage, between the two classes is much the same as in other counties.

† Spect. Feb. 12, 1876. "The New Domesday Book."

ably increased had the metropolitan district been included in the return.*

Lastly, according to a statement published in a recent number of the *Financial Reformer*, and referred to by Mr. Bright in a speech delivered at Rochdale last November, the number of owners of ten thousand acres and upwards in the United Kingdom is at present 955; and these gentlemen possess between them as nearly as possible 30,000,000† acres, or considerably more than one third of the entire computed acreage of Great Britain and Ireland. It would certainly be difficult to over-estimate the significance of these statistics; and when it is added that, according to the best obtainable information, at least seventy per cent. of the estates in this country are held under settlement, it will easily be seen that the difference is to be explained by the long continued prevalence amongst ourselves of the practice of entailing and the custom of primogeniture. The next point, as it would seem, which remains for consideration is the question whether the operation of this custom is so pernicious in its effects on the system of land tenure, and so injurious in its economical, social or political aspects—or in all these combined—as to imperatively require the interference of the legislature in the shape of a new land law.

Without reference to the teaching of experience, it does not seem from an *à priori* point of view that the state of things which confessedly exists in England—the concentration of rural property in the hands of comparatively few proprietors—is necessarily such as the economist must regard with disfavour, or more injurious than the inevitable ultimate consequences of any alternative system which the ingenuity of legislators could devise. One fatal objection to the existing system, already pointed out, of course does not exist in England; political privileges are not in the slightest degree associated with the ownership of land; and the occupier of the meanest tenement in a borough, or of

* Ibid, March 4, 1876.
† See a letter correcting a mistake in the figures from the Assistant Secretary to the Financial Reform Association in the *Times* Nov. 15 1877. The exact figure is 29,745,402.

half a dozen acres of soil in a rural district, has as much right to his representative in Parliament, and the same share in his return, as the owner of half a county. Putting this aside, there appear to be many reasons for considering the circumstance that land is a commodity mainly held in large quantities by men of wealth—often by men who would be richer if they possessed no land at all—as favourable to the utmost possible production and the highest development of the riches of the soil. The capitalist who owns land is able to introduce improvements, to venture on experiments and await his reward in the course of years to come; the petty occupier is obliged to grow what is immediately remunerative, and cannot afford to look beyond the necessities of the moment to the possibilities of the future. These conclusions certainly seem to be justified by facts, so far as they can be verified, and by figures, so far as they can be regarded as trustworthy. Let us compare for a moment the relative productiveness of the land in England and France. The soil of England is not on the whole better, or certainly not much better, suited to the growth of wheat than that of France. Yet Mr. McCulloch, writing nearly a generation ago, shews that the average crop of wheat per acre in England exceeded thirty and probably amounted to thirty-two bushels; while that of France did not in a good average year exceed fourteen bushels. One acre in England, it thus appears, yielded considerably more produce than two acres in France; and the conclusion irresistibly suggests itself that the difference must be chiefly explained by the adoption in this country of a better system of cultivation. If other kinds of grain, or wool, or beef, were taken as our standard, the result would have been still more decisively in our favour; and Mr. McCulloch further states that one man and one horse in England produced more grain and other agricultural produce than three men and a similar number of horses in France.[*] The same writer estimates two-thirds of the entire population of France to have been in 1847 engaged in agriculture, whence he infers

---

[*] Treatise on the Laws of Succession, &c., p. 117.

that two agriculturists supplied food for three persons, or for one beside themselves; while putting down the agricultural class in England as one-third of the population, it appears that with us two agriculturists supply food for no less than four persons besides themselves.* A table furnished by our representative in Prussia, Mr. Harris Gastrell, to the " Reports on Land Tenure " of Her Majesty's Representatives abroad,† published some seven years ago, while slightly altering these statistics—in particular, considerably reducing the proportion to the whole population borne by those engaged in agriculture in both countries, but especially in England,—fully corroborates Mr. McCulloch's view, and shews that while in England the percentage of persons engaged in agriculture is less than *half* the percentage of those similarly employed in any other country (excepting Holland) in Europe the average return of corn is more than double that obtained elsewhere, with the same exception in favour of Holland.‡ With regard to the tendency of occupiers, where the land is much subdivided, only to grow such crops as are immediately remunerative, it is instructive to observe how completely the Irish peasantry, where they have enjoyed a sort of customary tenant-right and a liberty of sub-letting and partitioning to an almost unlimited extent, have neglected all other cultivation for that of the potato; a similar phenomenon has been observed in France,§ in parts of

* Ibid, pp. 120, 121.
† Report on Land Tenure in Prussia, Land Tenure Reports, Vol. I., p. 221.

‡	Russia.	Italy.	France.	Belgium.	Prussia.	Austria.	Spain.	Holland.	United Kingdom
Percentage of agricultural to total population	85·90	77	51	51	45	25	25	16	12
Average return of corn per hectare	16	16	14·6	19·3	19·8	16	16	23	40·8

§ It appears from the official returns that the medium produce of the crops of potatoes in France during the seven years ending with 1824, amounted to about 40,517,000 hectolitres; whereas their average produce amounted, during

Belgium, and of Rhenish Prussia; and it is obvious that where such is the case the results of a temporary failure of the crop, produced perhaps by the unsuspected ravages of some destructive insect which defies extirpation, must always be viewed with the most serious apprehension. The proprietor of a couple of acres in Ireland or a single hectare in France, has little more to fall back upon, if his seed does not yield its increase, than the rice-growing ryot of Madras.

Numerous other evils resulting from excessive subdivision will readily suggest themselves and have often been pointed out. If the rural proprietor owns less land than a field of normal size—and good farming, steam ploughing, systematic manuring, etc., invariably imply fields of considerable extent—much of the soil will necessarily be wasted in superfluous hedges, injuring the cultivation in the vicinity, or in an excessive number of fences, the erection and repair of which must cause a heavy drain on the owner's purse. Another cause of waste consists in the large number of occupation roads or tracks which such a system requires; while it is almost needless to say that the best methods of cultivation cannot possibly be employed. Expensive manures and elaborate machinery are out of the small proprietor's reach; he has neither the intelligence to think of them, the money to pay for them, nor the skilled labour which their employment necessitates. In the matter of machinery, something it is true may be effected by co-operation; but not so much as is commonly supposed; since it will frequently happen that owing to the state of the weather, or the season of the year, the plough or the engine, to the expense of which all contribute, will be required by all at precisely the same time. It must moreover be remembered that the all-important principle of the division of labour, which political economy so strenuously inculcates, cannot possibly be applied

the seven years ending with 1835, to 63,951,000 hectolitres; being an increase in the interval of no less than 57 per cent. But the same returns shew that during the same interval the produce of wheat increased only 15 per cent., being a little more than a fourth part of the increase in the produce of potatoes; and we are informed that during the ten years ending with 1845, the increase in the produce of potatoes as compared with that of wheat was still greater.—McCulloch, *ut supra*, p. 122.

except in holdings of considerable extent. On a large estate, one man may make a speciality of hedging and ditching, another of ploughing and harrowing, a third of thrashing or manuring, a fourth of superintending the live stock, and so on; where the acreage is small, the same man must learn as well as he can to do everything, and will waste a large proportion of his time in attaining a very indifferent degree of aptitude for each branch of agriculture. There is another point which, in estimating the relative advantages of large and small proprietors, certainly should not be left out of sight. I refer to the preservation of timber, which becomes almost impossible when the land is divided into a large number of minute holdings, and which is to a great extent insured in the case of settled land in England by the prohibition of waste on the part of a life tenant. That a judicious protection of timber and restrictions on its indiscriminate destruction are indispensable to the prosperity of a country, and not merely to its ornament and beauty, are propositions which scarcely require demonstration; and the statement that timber is rapidly disappearing in many parts of France, and even in those mountainous districts where it is most urgently needed both for shelter and for the protection of the lower soil, is one which every traveller can verify for himself. It would indeed be absurd to expect the small proprietor, when free to act as he pleases without restriction from the law, to appreciate such considerations, and sacrifice the immediate advantages accruing from an abundant supply of fuel, from the sale of such timber as he does not himself require, and from the extension of his cultivable area, to the ultimate well-being of an estate which in the course of a couple of generations will be divided into a dozen fractions.*

Our own system of entails does not, it need scarcely be said, present any obstacle to the creation or preservation of small holdings where the condition of the soil renders them

* I am informed that where a good system of woodcraft is employed it is often more profitable, even directly, to keep land under timber than to convert it into arable or pasture. In many cases where, if so converted, it would not let for more than thirty shillings an acre, the mere sale of superfluous timber and underwood brings in a clear forty shillings. This of course can only be realized where the wood is of considerable extent.

desirable; on the other hand, it seems certain that the summary abolition of such a system and the substitution for it of a law of compulsory partition—which must inevitably be applied equally to all estates, the smallest as well as the greatest—would in the end render the existence of any but small holdings impossible. It may be worth while, though the point is one rather of historical and political than of economical interest, to briefly point out the circumstances under which the system of *morcellement*, introduced by France and to a great extent copied by most of the leading States in Europe first arose in the former country.

The *Code Napoléon*, and the law of succession which it introduced, was one of the results—from one point of view perhaps the most important result—of the Revolution which preceded it. The land-law which it contains was indeed first enacted in 1791. It has been well pointed out that this law was not in the main dictated by any considerations of public interest or economical expediency, but by the determination of the people to finally crush the power of the nobility and avenge themselves for all the oppression which during so many generations they had suffered at their hands. In attaining this object, narrow as it was, the revolutionary legislators were completely successful. The ancestral nobility, as a social force, ceased to exist; and it cannot be denied that the *noblesse*, as an institution, amply deserved its doom. The contrast between the gradual and pacific manner in which the obnoxious characteristics of feudalism were removed in England, and the violent and summary fashion in which they were swept off the face of the land in France, and the causes which produced so striking a difference, form the subject of a most valuable and suggestive essay recently published by Sir Henry Maine.[*] The French nobility at the end of the last century had lost all their political power; but it unfortunately happened that they had retained all their private privileges, and had not abated in the slightest degree their proprietary pretensions. France was no longer governed by the King and Parliaments

[*] *Fortnightly Review*, April 1, 1877. The Decay of Feudal Property in France and England.

but by the King alone; but all the oppressive rights of feudalism—of which the last vestige had disappeared from England on the Restoration—were still claimed and exercised by the class of hereditary nobles. This divorce of private rights from public responsibility has happily never been witnessed in our country; it is indeed no exaggeration to describe their combination as the real keystone of our landed system, and the best security for its preservation. But before the French revolution, the nobles were regarded by the class of peasant proprietors as mere *fruges consumere nati*; and the latter were in much the same condition, as Sir Henry Maine observes, as that which an English copyholder might theoretically occupy, in a manor where all the most vexatious characteristics of that system of tenure were not merely nominally united, but in practice rigorously enforced. The *corvées*, or compulsory service of the peasantry on every possible pretext, the iniquitous and irritating burdens of such rights as the *droit de colombier* and *droit de guarenne*, bear a strong resemblance to the most objectionable privileges ever claimed by the lord of a copyhold manor; while the monopoly of grinding corn can only be paralleled by the oppressive regulations, with the same object, which Tacitus describes the Roman provincial authorities as having devised in Spain. It was against oppression of this kind that the peasants at length rose *en masse* and ensured the success of the Revolution. In the year 1789 there occurred those outbreaks of incendiary violence which are sometimes spoken of as " the burning of the chateaux." It is remarkable that in almost every case their first proceeding on attacking the mansion of a noble was to proceed to the muniment-room and destroy the title deeds, on which these pretensions were invariably based; a practice which continued until the promulgation of the new land-law rendered their revival impossible.* It was under circumstances such

---

* The title deeds of the lord had become of the greatest importance, and the advantage which the tenants gained by their destruction is obvious enough. At a later date it lost its value in the eyes of the peasantry, because more drastic remedies for their grievances had then been devised. The legislation of the Constituent Assembly swept away the greatest part of the feudal dues and

as these, and not through any considerations of State policy, that the custom of primogeniture was abolished in France, and a law of equal succession established in its place. Other countries through various causes were led to follow the example of France, and at the present day the system of *légitime*—limiting the property of which an owner can dispose at his pleasure, if he have lineal descendants, and usually also if he have lineal ancestors, to from one-third to one-half of his whole estate, and establishing the principle of compulsory and equal succession by the lineal representatives to the remaining portion—subsists, among other European countries, in Austria, Bavaria, Belgium, Denmark, France, Germany, Holland, Italy, Norway, Portugal and Spain. In many of these countries all entails have been abolished; in others those existing on the change in the land-laws were respected but their future creation strictly prohibited.*

It is somewhat curious to observe that the French succession law—the adoption of which has often been advocated as a panacea for the evils of entail—has itself produced almost all the disadvantages inherent in a system of perpetual entails. Not the eldest son only, but all the sons, are to a great extent independent of the parental authority, since they know that parental displeasure cannot affect their pecuniary expectations; while the owner of an estate which he cannot dispose of at will, and which he knows must on his death be necessarily broken up, is deprived of the most powerful incentives to enterprise and accumulation, and can feel but little disposition to effect any improvements of which he is not certain to reap the benefit in person.

---

provided compensation for only a part of them. The Legislative or Second Assembly abolished the residue and withdrew the compensation. The Convenvention or Third, found almost nothing to destroy, though it was passionately eager to fasten on a hated institution, and though the Revolutionary lawyers, who abounded in it, were the real authors of the legislative provisions afterwards engrafted on the Code Napoléon, which for ever prevented the revival of feudal ownership in France.—Maine, *Fortnightly Review*, vol. 27, p. 463.

* For full particulars and statistics on these points see a work on " The Succession Laws of Christian Countries with special reference to the law of primogeniture as it exists in England ;" by Mr. Eyre Lloyd ; London, 1877.

The severe restraints on the testamentary power imposed by the *Code Napoléon* have in fact, in the words of Sir Henry Maine, " established a system of small perpetual entails, which is infinitely nearer akin to the system of feudal Europe than would be a perfect liberty of bequest. Feeling and opinion in this country [England] have been profoundedly affected by the practice of free testamentary disposition; and it appears to me that the state of sentiment in a great part of French society, on the subject of the conservation of property in families, is much liker that which prevailed throughout Europe two or three centuries ago than are the current opinions of Englishmen."*

It is almost universally admitted that the practice of *morcellement* in France has by this time gone far enough; but as De Tocqueville explained in forcible and eloquent language, forty years ago, the machinery which a law of succession when once adopted puts into motion is not easily arrested or retarded, but constantly gathers an increased momentum in its progress. " Ce n'est pas sans doute à nous, Français du xixe siècle, témoins journaliers des changemens politiques et sociaux que la loi des successions fait naître, à mettre en doute son pouvoir. Chaque jour, nous la voyons passer et repasser sans cesse sur notre sol, renversant sur son chemin les murs de nos demeures, et détruisant la clôture de nos champs. Mais si la loi des successions a déjà beaucoup fait parmi nous, beaucoup lui reste encore à faire. Nos souvenirs, nos opinions et nos habitudes, lui opposent de puissans obstacles."† Of the " much which still remained " at the time when these lines were penned for the law of succession to effect, the most part has been accomplished; and the powerful obstacles which memory, opinions, and habits once presented to its operation, no longer have any substantial existence.‡ Mr. Sackville West, who furnished

* Ancient Law, pp. 226, 227.

† De la Démocratie en Amérique. Vol. I. pp. 81, 82.

‡ " Occasionally, indeed, the few individuals who have not got wholly rid of aristocratical prejudices endeavour, by accumulating monied property, to provide portions for their younger children, so that the land may descend entire to the eldest son. But, except in the case of a few of the greater proprietors, or of those who are manufacturers or traders as well as land-

the Report on Land Tenure in France, in answer to the Foreign Office circular of the late government, while not insensible to the advantages, both political and agricultural, of a large class of small proprietors, adds his complete concurrence in M. Lavergne's opinion that *morcellement* cannot be carried further without danger, and that " an unlimited partition of the small properties as they already exist would be productive of serious evil." Mr. McCulloch had quoted the official statistics, procured for the assessment of the *contribution foncière*, to shew that there were only 53,000 properties in France worth upwards of £200 a year; and we gather from Mr. Sackville West's report that at the beginning of the present decade out of seven million and a half proprietors about five million held on an average only six acres each, while only 50,000 averaged 600 acres. " With some rare exceptions," he adds, " all the great properties have been gradually broken up, and even the first and second classes—those averaging 600 and 60 acres respectively—are fast merging into the third." In France, a farm of a couple of hundred acres is placed in the class of " large properties "; and notwithstanding the enormous

owners, this is all but impossible; and the longer the law continues, the weaker will be the principle that prompts to such conduct. Indeed, though ardently sought for by the poorer classes, real is at present held in less estimation by the more opulent portion of the community, than personal property. A landowner, without something like an equivalent monied fortune, knows, if he have more than one child, that his estate will, most likely, be sold or subdivided at his death; and having this knowledge, he regards it merely as a transitory possession, and takes comparatively little interest in its condition. He neither builds a mansion, lays out a park, nor undertakes many of the numerous improvements he might have undertaken had he felt sure his estate would continue entire. His vanity is not flattered, nor his industry stimulated, by the hope of founding or perpetuating a family; but he must anticipate, even though he have only one son, that his property and his descendants will be ultimately, and at no very remote period, merged in the indistinguishable mass of petty patches and occupiers. Hence, while the law of succession weakens on the one hand the motives to industry, it tends, on the other, to level and obliterate all distinctions of family and wealth. But the evil is, that the equality it introduces is not brought about by the exaltation of the poor, but by the depression of the rich. It is hostile to both classes, and nearly in the same degree."—McCulloch, pp. 86, 87. These remarks, to a great extent justified by the state of affairs thirty years ago, are fully confirmed by the process which has gone on with incessant rapidity since that date.

subdivision of land, subletting to tenant occupiers is extremely prevalent. The demand for patches of land is so great that an owner of 60 to 200 acres finds it far less profitable to farm them all himself than to divide them into small patches, which are let to the highest bidder; a system which perhaps tends more rapidly than any other to exhaust the soil, and which presents the most insuperable obstacle to agricultural progress and the development of good husbandry. According to the statement of M. de Chateauvieux, an agricultural and statistical writer whom Mr. McCulloch regards as trustworthy, no less than 35,000,000 acres in France—or an extent of land nearly equivalent to the entire acreage of all England and Wales—are farmed on the *metayer* system!

All that can be said for the present condition of property in France and its effect on agriculture has been excellently put by Mr. Cliffe Leslie in his Essay on the French System, written for the volume published by the Cobden Club;* he is indeed successful in shewing that the price of land in France has greatly risen with the increase of small properties, that the extent to which such properties are encumbered by debt may have been to some extent exaggerated, and that there are several branches of agricultural industry, such as dairy farming, market gardening and the raising of cattle for the market, for which the soil of France is in some districts admirably adapted, and which *la petite culture* has developed to an extent which would have been otherwise impossible. But it is admitted that the proportion of soil utilised for these purposes does not exceed one-fifteenth of the whole;† and with regard to the price of land, it is scarcely a healthy economical sign that through adventitious causes, and the ruinous competition of small proprietors, it should be abnormally inflated. The fact that land fetches more than it is really worth, and is thus placed out of the reach of all but the wealthy few, is indeed one of the characteristics of the English conditions of tenure which is most often

---

* The Land System of France : by J. E. Cliffe Leslie. Systems of Land Tenure, pp. 335-367.

† Ibid : p. 342.

and most vehemently, but very inconsistently, attacked by the panegyrists of the French system. It may be added that the keen demand for small plots of ground tends at once to artificially increase the price of land and to accelerate the progress of *morcellement*. Garnier, the French translator of the *Wealth of Nations*, states that a farm of which the rental would be about £200 a year, if sold as a whole will not fetch more than twenty-five years purchase; but if sold in small lots it will obtain something like forty years purchase. It naturally follows that estates of any size when brought into the market are almost invariably subdivided into small patches before being offered for sale.*

Enough has been said to shew that the evil consequences which in the course of little more than two generations have been produced by the French system are such as to call urgently for a remedy. Such a remedy, as it would seem, could be found only in the abolition of the law of compulsory partition; and this is a step which while the state of feeling in France continues as at present cannot possibly be expected and which, it is greatly to be feared, if ever adopted will come too late to arrest the mischievous consequences of the existing law. Further proof of the view which I have felt obliged to take will be found, if required, in Mr. McCulloch's admirable treatise on the Laws of Succession. It may however be worth while, before leaving this portion of the subject, to point out how little the expectations of those who defended the French law from a theoretical point of view before time had given an opportunity of estimating its practical consequences have been realised in fact.

Mr. John Austin, writing in 1824 in the *Westminster Review*, expressed himself as not in principle in favour of the French law of compulsory division, on the somewhat singular ground that its ultimate tendency was to produce not equality, but inequality in property.† He advocated a free liberty of

---

* *Richesse des Nations*, VI. 179, ed. 1822 : quoted by McCulloch.

† Mr. Austin expresses an opinion that the free power of testamentary disposition tends in the end more certainly to the establishment of approximate equality than any restraints placed on that power with a view to such end ; p. 504. This opinion does not seem to be justified by experience.

testamentary bequest, coupled with an entire prohibition of substitutions or entails; but he at the same time took occasion to deny that the natural consequences of the law of succession are such as Mr. McCulloch, in an article published in the *Edinburgh Review* during the same year, had predicted, and as the latter writer was able afterwards to shew, in his later and more elaborate treatise, had been actually realised by contemporary experience. The grounds of Mr. Austin's dissent are certainly singular, and would seem to have originated in his profound belief in the influence over the common actions of ordinary mankind of those philosophical principles of utility to which he was so warmly attached, and of which he lost no opportunity to propound and inculcate the general applicability. Mr. Austin, after intimating his agreement with the opinion that large holdings augment the productiveness of agricultural labour and capital, and adding some very striking and valuable arguments in support of that opinion,* proceeds to deny that the existence of a law of compulsory partition necessarily or even probably involves an excessive subdivision of landed properties. How does he arrive at this startling conclusion? He shews that on the children acquiring, on their father's decease, the paternal estate in equal shares, it lies in their power either to divide it into separate portions, to retain it undivided and carry on its management in partnership, to lease the whole farm to one of the brothers or to a stranger, to sell it to a stranger, and divide the proceeds, or lastly to sell it to one among themselves, the latter, if not prepared with the purchase money, giving his co-heirs a mortgage on the estate. The reviewer then proceeds to shew, or to attempt to shew, that any one of the latter courses would be in the view of economical science more expedient than that first mentioned; and immediately concludes from this circumstance that the course of equal partition will be in practice rarely if ever adopted. "To determine what they would do," he says, "let us ascertain what it would be their interest to do. If they would not

* See *Westminster Review*, Oct. 1824, pp. 514-516.

probably do what it would be their interest to do, it follows that human conduct can never be anticipated, and the proud structure of economical science falls at once to the ground."

This general proposition may be said to partake of the nature at once of a sophism and of a truism. If it be merely meant that the actions of the average individual are usually dictated by what he himself conceives to be his interest—and if we include in the expression "interest" the idea of *duty*, an idea which, whether mistaken or not, certainly exercises no inconsiderable influence on the actions of a large proportion of mankind—there can be no hesitation in accepting Mr. Austin's axiom. If, however, he means that the ideas of his interest, and the notions of what is expedient, entertained by an uninstructed peasant are invariably, or even usually, identical with those of the politician, the philosopher or the political economist, the proposition is one of which the mere statement is sufficient to demonstrate the absurdity. The peasant proprietor is influenced by a thousand considerations, by attachment to the soil on which he has always lived, by family ties and long established friendships, by ignorance of the world, by absence of education and unfamiliarity with any other pursuit than that of agriculture, above all by what may be best described as a *vis inertiæ* which operates with him more powerfully than with any other class, circumstances all of which taken together have more than sufficient weight to prevail over any ultimate balance of pecuniary interest which is all that the economist can regard. Political economy, as has been well remarked, is a science of abstraction; and the process which it involves often by its operation casts aside facts and data which cannot be neglected without gravely diminishing the value of the solutions which that science supplies of the curious problems to which it is applied. It may be all very well to take utility as the ultimate standard of the philosopher, but the assumption that ordinary people habitually act up to a philosopher's view of what is useful is almost grotesquely incongruous with the teaching of experience. It would certainly have been far more satisfactory if Mr. Austin, instead of founding an elaborate argument as to the probable conduct of the small rural proprietor on what, in the writer's opinion, was the interest of the latter, had turned his attention to what as a matter of fact was the habitual conduct of that class; and had he pursued such an inquiry with impartiality and care, we can scarcely doubt that he would have found that his *à priori* theories required considerable modification in order to adjust them to the teaching of actual facts. As an instance of the curious results to which Mr. Austin's method led him, it may be mentioned that he arrived at the conclusion that owing to the increase of wealth and accumulation of capital in France, small farms would in time be to a great extent superseded by larger occupations.* As a matter of fact, enough has been said above to show that the reverse process has been going on with progressive rapidity ever since the day when Austin wrote.

It should also be noticed that the fancied security of the French peasant proprietors seems to exist mainly in the imagination of enthusiastic panegyrists of the French system. We may indeed well doubt whether the peasant is at the present day really more secure in his occupation than he was before the Revolution, although none would question the enormous benefit and addition to his material prosperity which he has otherwise derived from his deliverance from the oppressive exactions of the feudal *seigneur*. Many of the small proprietors live, it is notorious, in a condition of chronic embarrassment, partly no doubt produced by their eagerness to purchase plots of land, even, if necessary, with borrowed money. "A large proportion of the owners," says Mr. McCulloch, " are barely able, with all their proverbial parsimony, to discharge the interest of the sums secured upon the land, and are wholly without the means of attempting any improvement, or even of recovering from an accidental calamity, such as a hail-storm or an inundation."† He goes on to show that in 1832 the amount of mortgage

* *Westminster Review, ut supra*, p. 531.
† Treatise on Succession, p. 106.

debts in France was no less than 11,233,000,000fr., while in 1847 it had reached at a moderate estimate no less than 14,000,000,000fr. The interest on this principal would amount to twenty-eight millions *sterling*, if calculated at five per cent.; but it seems that the rate of interest really varies from six to ten per cent. Such being the figures, we are not surprised to learn that great numbers of small properties are annually sold to satisfy the demands of creditors; and when we are told that more than one half of the property in the United Kingdom is under mortgage—a statement which on the authority of Mr. Joshua Williams we must probably accept—we may still consider ourselves entitled to ask, by the light of these statistics, whether the opposite system, as pursued in France, has been more successful in preserving the land from the burden of such incumbrances.

There are two significant facts with the mere statement of which we may conclude a comparative examination, already it is to be feared unduly long. The principles of free trade, which France at one time seemed to have definitely adopted, are falling more and more into disfavour in that country. The manufacturing and agricultural interests concur in demanding a larger measure of protection; and it does not seem rash to attribute this retrograde step in some degree to the incapacity of a land, fettered by such pernicious conditions of tenure, to compete on equal terms with the greater fertility and productiveness of other countries, of which the industry has never been hampered by such a disastrous system. Once more, the prosperity of a country may be roughly measured by the increase of population. The test is, of course, by no means infallible; since the growth of population may be sensibly retarded by adventitious circumstances—such as war, famine or internal revolution—of which the operation is merely temporary. So far as it goes however the criterion is a good one; and it is not a little remarkable that, as far as can be ascertained, the population of France within the last decade so far from increasing in the same ratio as in England and Germany—

notwithstanding the fact that the land-system and policy of both these countries are distinctly favourable to emigration and colonization, to an extent unknown in France—so far from increasing in the same proportion as in other countries with easier outlets for their superfluous inhabitants, has been entirely stationary, if not actually retrogressive.* The attention of politicians has recently been directed to this grave phenomenon; but I venture to suggest that it is only a natural, probably an inevitable, consequence of a law of succession which practically roots the people to an unelastic area of cultivable land.

It would be foreign to the purpose of this essay, and would extend it to a tedious length, were I to attempt to shew that the same causes as in France, so far as they have been left unchecked, have in other European countries produced very similar results. The impression however that France is the only country in which subdivision has been carried to an injurious extent would be altogether erroneous. In Prussia the old feudal system was originally abolished in order to increase the defensive power of the population; and the measure was highly successful in attaining its immediate object.† The evils however resulting from an excessive multiplication of small properties were not long in manifesting themselves; and a proposal to introduce the law of Primogeniture into the succession to certain classes of property was seriously discussed at the first meeting of the Prusian diet in 1847. Nothing however was done in that direction; and, according to Mr. Harris Gastrell's recent report, out of about 185,000 properties in the province

* It appears from the census-returns recently published that there has been in the last five years a very slight increase in the population of France; but it is almost exclusively confined to the large towns, and in many of the most purely agricultural districts there has been a positive decrease. Moreover, such addition as there has been is in great measure to be attributed to an extensive immigration from Alsace and Lorraine.

† An excellent account of the Prussian agrarian legislation of 1807, 1811 and 1850, is given in the paper contributed by Mr. R. B. D. Morier, C.B. (now Her Majesty's Minister at Lisbon) to *Systems of Land Tenure in Various Countries*: see especially pp. 297-326.

H

of Prussia rather more than one half do not exceed twenty acres in extent.*

Turning to Wurtemburg, we find it reported as being "the country where subdivision of land is carried to the greatest extent." In that state there are 280,000 peasant proprietors with not more than five acres each, and only about 160,000 estates exceeding five acres in extent. In Wurtemburg however the *légitime* does not exceed a third of the whole property, unless where the children are at least four in number; and it is certainly remarkable that even this moderate application of the *legitim* principle, together with the law of equal succession on intestacy, has been capable of carrying sub-division to so great an extent. Efforts have in fact been made to check its spread by the introduction among the peasant proprietors of customs which though scarely consistent with the law are not interfered with by the Courts. The eldest son usually succeeds by the father's will to the whole of the paternal land, and his brothers and sisters receive a pecuniary compensation for their exclusion, which rarely, if ever, amounts to the share which they would have acquired on an equal division of the estate. "The daughters, however," writes the author of the official report, "are more frequently on their marriage allotted an equal share of land, and, as the husband is probably the proprietor of a piece of land elsewhere in the commune, the intersection and subdivision of the land goes on increasing." It should also be mentioned, as another consequence of the partition system in Wurtemburg, that the number of marriages is much restricted by communal regulations and that, as a natural result, the increase of the legitimate population, as compared with that in other parts of Germany, has been of late years extremely small.† The law and its practical results are much the same in Bavaria. The former prescribes equal partition; but a system of

* On the customs by which the law of succession is to some extent counteracted in East and West Prussia, Silesia, and Pomerania cf. Mr. Eyre Lloyd's *Laws of Succession &c.*, pp. 63, 64.

† See Land Tenure Report: Part I.; Eyre Lloyd, pp. 82, 83; Cobden Club Essays, pp. 79, 80.

Primogeniture has been introduced by custom. "In short," writes Mr. Brodrick, "the peasant proprietors of Bavaria, who are admitted to be a thriving class, appear to keep up their family estates with as much tenacity as our own landed gentry, but with a jealousy for the rights of younger children which reminds us of the Irish peasant farmers."*

In Austria, however, the regulations of the *code civile* are rigorously maintained, and no preference is accorded to the eldest sons. Entails for the benefit of the latter, or of other relatives, called according to the nature of the instrument a Primogeniture, majorat, or seniorat—in which latter case the eldest relation of the same degree succeeds—are however occasionally permitted, but require a special charter and a legislative sanction, which forcibly reminds us of the old patrician will of the Comitia Calata. The feudal system was abolished in Austria by the land laws of 1848-49, when the peasant was converted, as previously in France and more recently in Russia, from a predial serf into a free and independent proprietor of the soil. The result of the present system may be best described by a brief extract from the official report made by Her Majesty's representative in Austria, the present Viceroy of India, in reply to the circular of the foreign office. Lord Lytton says:—

"Whilst recognising a vast improvement in the social and intellectual standard of the Austrian peasantry since 1848, he is constrained to observe that there can be no doubt whatever that every impulse in the way of agricultural improvement has come exclusively from the great landowners . . . . it is a notorious and striking fact that in the most agricultural empire of Austria, agriculture only flourishes in those provinces where great estates and great landowners prevail; and in all those parts of the country where the peasant proprietor predominates, the state of agriculture is singularly rude and primitive."†

In Belgium the practice of *morcellement* has been carried even further than in France itself; the average size of estates, exclusive of woodlands and wastes, has been estimated at seven acres; and Mr. Grattan shews from official statistics that four-fifths of the farms did not exceed twelve acres in extent. The amount of cultivable land held in large hold-

* Cobden Club Essays, p. 81.
† Land Tenure Reports: Part II., p. 29.

ings would appear to be small and constantly decreasing; and, as in France, the process of subdivision is accelerated by the practice of breaking up estates, when brought into the market, into small parcels. Mr. Wyndham, Secretary to the Britannic Legation, reporting in 1869, remarks as follows:—

"I have heard the opinion expressed by a person thoroughly conversant with the agricultural status of Belgium that the excessive subdivision was injurious to agriculture, and a regret expressed that there was no law preventing the subdivision of properties of 15 hectares in extent. The law regulating the equal partition of property, though it breaks up large properties, equally affects the small. The death of parents, who, through their toil and industry, have succeeded in saving sufficient money to purchase a small house and a few hectares of land, entails in all probability the sale of the property, in order to carry into effect the division, as laid down by law, amongst the family; sometimes an arrangement is arrived at by which one or two of the sons keep the home and land, paying an indemnity to their brothers or sisters; but this is a matter of difficulty, and children of parents who have raised themselves to the position of small proprietors are all reduced at the death of the parents to the humble position from which the latter started."*

On the other hand, it is very remarkable that while Holland is the only country in Europe, as appears from the tabular statement cited above, which compares at all favourably with England in the productiveness of its soil and in the proportion of the population which agriculture leaves free to acquire and manufacture wealth in other ways, the feeling in that country is strongly opposed to unnecessary subdivision of estates.† The rule of the law is the same as in France and Belgium; but it has been in great measure counteracted by public opinion and the good sense and forethought of individuals. "It is a common thing," writes Mr. Locock, in his contribution to the official reports on Land Tenure, "for a farmer, whether proprietor or tenant, to have accumulated before his death sufficient movable property, frequently in the funds, to enable him to assign a portion therefrom"—*i.e.*, the amount required by the Succession Law—"to one or another of his children."

* Land Tenure Reports, part ii., p. 235.
† Land Tenure Reports, part i., p. 214.

In Italy and Portugal the system of compulsory division prevails; and of the latter country we learn that it is the prevalent opinion that " where, as is frequently the case, the subdivision of land has been carried to excess, the result has been to lower the standard of living of the rural population."[*] The same remark is doubtless equally applicable to Italy. In Spain however a large portion of the territory is in the hands of the grandees and subject to entail; lands belonging to the clergy are also inalienable; and the law of equal partition is therefore of comparatively small importance.[†]

Enough has been said to shew that the system of compulsory partition, originally produced in almost every case rather by political than economical considerations, while it may perhaps have some advantage in *temporarily* improving the condition of the peasantry, is, even from that point of view, ultimately deplorable in its results; while, considered in its economical aspect, its effects are almost uniformly inimical to agricultural improvement. It would not however be candid to assume that this is the only system which opponents of the practice of settlement have suggested in its place. A more specious suggestion, advocated by Mr. John Austin in the above-mentioned article in the *Westminster Review*, and more recently by Mr. Fowler, formerly member for Cambridge, in a paper on " The present aspect of the land question," is that while entails should be abolished the present free liberty of conveyance and bequest, unrestricted by law, should be uniformly retained. It is proposed to convert all existing estates into fee-simple, and to prohibit the transfer by deed or will of any smaller estate than that which the possessor himself enjoys. The question to be considered is whether the evils of entail are so great as to render such a change desirable, notwithstanding the objectionable features which it presents. That it would be in many respects objectionable is not difficult to prove. If indeed it were merely proposed to limit the

[*] Land Tenure Reports, part i., p. 171.
[†] Eyre Lloyd, *ut supra*, p. 70.

practice of entailing and to assimilate the law to that, for instance, which prevails in most of the states of the American Union, where the power of checking alienation has been restricted to the creation of *two* successive life estates, limited to lives in being at the time of the execution of the instrument, there would be no reason to regard such a suggestion with grave alarm. It probably would not seriously affect the existing system of tenure, deeply rooted as it is in the feelings, perhaps in the prejudices, of our landed proprietors; and its principal result would be that arrangements for re-settlement would be effected with greater frequency than is at present necessary. But the total abolition of entails would produce consequences of a very different and a much more serious kind. In the first place, such a change in the law would certainly provoke the most violent opposition on the part of the class which would be mainly affected by its operation. It may indeed well be questioned whether in the face of the sentiments on this subject, the offspring of long-continued custom—and custom which is believed on the whole to have worked satisfactorily—which are known to prevail, so sweeping an alteration would be even feasible; and it seems still more difficult to feel assured that if feasible it would be also expedient. A land-law of which the immediate operation would be felt by a particular class alone, and which the class in question would to a man resent, can be justified only by the gravest social or economical necessity, the existence of both or either of which appears to the present writer to require further proof. Neither can it be asserted that the objection of the landed class to the abolition of the law of entail rests on merely sentimental grounds. It would inevitably tend, and its advocates do not conceal their expectation that it would tend, to the disruption of large estates. Now the existence of such estates, as has been shewn above, seems to have formed a necessary condition of agricultural progress in the past, and certainly at the present day when, owing to the introduction of machinery and improved methods of cultivation, good farming constantly tends to involve a more liberal application of capital and a larger measure of intelligence, their destruction cannot be regarded as an event which the economist would regard with satisfaction. At the same time, it is perfectly certain that they cannot be permanently maintained by any other method than the practice of entail at present in use. If every tenant held the fee simple of his estate, the energy and self-sacrifice of a dozen generations of admirable landlords would be always liable to be dissipated by the imprudence or extravagance of a single descendant. Family pride may or may not be in itself a virtue, but there is assuredly no greater incentive to exertion and to thrift; and the motive to the exercise of these qualities involved in the hope of perpetuating a family and a name would be immensely attenuated by rendering any such perpetuity an idle dream or impossible chimera. It has indeed been urged that a class which is too weak and thoughtless to be capable of protecting itself has no right to invoke the protection of the law against its dissolution; an argument which those who employ would certainly hesitate to extend in a logical manner to all parallel cases. The law is generally regarded as performing not the least useful of its functions when it protects the weak not only from external injustice, but from the disastrous effects of their own actions, when these effects are not confined to the actual agents alone. The theory however seems still more inappropriate when it is remembered that as matters at present stand the landed proprietor asks for no aid from the Courts except the common right of every subject in the realm—the due enforcement of contracts, the interpretation where necessary of ambiguities in their phraseology, and the protection of property against injury and trespass. What is proposed is no less than a direct interference, by legislative act, with freedom of contract in dealing with the soil. It has been already conceded that in certain conceivable cases such interference may be justifiable and even praiseworthy, but only when exercised as a *pis aller*, and in the last resort. What then are those characteristics of the system of entails so inherent in that system and so vicious in their results as to imperatively require its summary destruction?

The grounds on which the practice is attacked are briefly as follows. It is said to interfere to a vexatious extent with the liberty of the landlord, and to render him sometimes unable and sometimes unwilling to manage his estate to the best advantage; it is also alleged that it exercises an unfavourable influence on the position of the tenant, diminishes his security, discourages him from making necessary improvements, and adds to the difficulties of his relations with the owner. It is moreover urged that the circumstance that so large a proportion of the land is strictly tied up under settlement has practically taken the soil of the country out of the category of marketable commodities, and prevented intending purchasers from gratifying a reasonable and honourable desire to become owners of freehold estates.*

Let us proceed to consider these objections in the order above laid down. It is often urged that the tenant for life who, under a settlement or will, and much more frequently by the former instrument, comes into possession may well happen to be completely ignorant of agriculture and to have little taste for a country life; and that the land is thus prevented from coming into the hands of those who would turn it to the best account, while to the other evils of bad management those of absenteeism may be added. The evils of absenteeism are no doubt from a social standpoint very considerable; from an economical point of view, and considered in themselves alone, they have probably been much exaggerated. The landlord, whether resident or not, has usually the strongest pecuniary inducement to turn his estate to the best account; it is seldom difficult to select a

* An interesting discussion on the subject of entails took place in the House of Commons in April, 1872, on a motion by Mr. W. Fowler "That in the opinion of this House the present state of the Law as to the entail and strict settlement of land discourages the investment of capital in the development of agriculture, to the great injury of all classes of the people, and increases the complication of titles, and the expense and delay incident to the transfer of real estate." Mr. Gladstone recommended Mr. Fowler not to press his motion to a division: in the result it was negatived by 103 to 81. (Hansard, ccx., pp. 991-1031). A proposition of the same kind in the present Parliament would doubtless meet with a still more decisive defeat.

competent steward or agent for that purpose; and it has been observed that the best managed estates are very frequently those where the landlord, perhaps a great nobleman taking a leading part in public life, has very slight personal acquaintance with agriculture, and where he is in the habit of residing for perhaps less than a month in the year. It will however be rejoined that, even granting this to be true, the landlord's interest being only of a temporary character, he has the strongest temptation to exhaust the soil, and will assuredly be disinclined to lay out large sums of money on improvements which do not promise any immediate return. Experience does not prove this theory to be correct; and it certainly seems to leave out of sight the circumstance that in the vast majority of cases the devolution of estates under settlement is the same as the tenant in possession, if owning the fee-simple, would himself prescribe. In such cases it is obvious that the law of entail will not affect his actions; and moreover there are very few improvements of such a nature that he who effects them may not hope to derive in consequence substantial benefit in the course of a few years; while there are very few individuals who do not think themselves justified in anticipating a further lease of life of similar duration. Lastly, it is important to remember that most real improvements, tending to increase the productiveness of the soil, are under the English system naturally effected not by the landlord but by the tenant; and this brings us to the second point—the assertion that the present state of the law is discouraging to the energies of the tenant, and by making his footing precarious presents an obstacle to his adopting any methods of cultivation of which he cannot reckon on immediately reaping the fruit.

The old system by which a tenant was required, as a condition of preserving his holding, to pay an arbitrary fine —now restricted to two years' value—on the death of the landlord, at present only exists in the case of copyholders, who are really not tenants but proprietors, and proprietors whose land is being rapidly enfranchised, under the provision of a recent Act, by the action of commissioners.* The great grievance involved in the settling of estates has been that it frequently involved the deprival of the tenant in possession of all power of leasing; for no tenant for life could grant a farmer a lease unless a special power to that effect was inserted, as was the case with all well-drawn deeds, in the deed of settlement; and the inferior tenant being thus at any moment liable to eviction, on the demise of the superior, was placed in a most unsatisfactory position. In Scotland, under the system of perpetual entails, the case was much the same; an entailer might there prohibit the granting of any lease, however short, and the charging the estate with debts, even when contracted for the most necessary improvements. More than a century ago, conditions of this kind had produced such great inconvenience as to call for a legislative remedy; and by an Act of George III., entitled "An Act for the Improvement of Lands, &c.,"† a tenant in possession was empowered to grant leases for ninety-nine years for building purposes, and for fourteen years and one existing life, or for thirty-one years, for agricultural purposes; and to burden the estate to an extent not exceeding six years' rent for improvements of a nature specified in the Act. The House of Lords subsequently pronounced the practice of taking fines or *grassums*, at the commencement of a lease, illegal; and since that decision the farmers on an entailed estate in Scotland have been in scarcely any respect worse off than on those not similarly limited.‡

In England an Act was passed in 1856, entitled an Act to facilitate leases and sales of settled estates,§ which provided that when the instrument by which any settled estate was limited was made after that act came into force, and did not contain any express provisions to the contrary, any tenant for life might grant leases of any portion of the

* St. 15 and 16 Vict., c. 51, amended by St. 21 and 22 Vict., c. 94.
† St. 10 Geo. III., c. 51 (The Montgomery Act).
‡ See McCulloch, *ut supra*, pp. 66, 67.
§ St. 19 and 20. Vict. c. 120.

estate for any term not exceeding twenty-one years provided that the best rent that could reasonably be obtained was reserved, that no fine was raised, and that the usual covenants as to payment and re-entry were inserted. It was also provided that, whatever the date of the settlement, leases might be granted on the authority of the Court of Chancery for terms not exceeding 21 years for an agricultural, 40 years for a mining, &c., 60 years for a repairing, and 99 years for a building lease. The operation of this Act has been, as far as can be judged, on the whole eminently satisfactory; it provides to some extent for the event of accidental omission, a contingency which however hardly ever occurs, of powers intended to be granted by the deed of settlement, while at the same time it does not substantially interfere with the liberty of drawing up such instruments of entail as may seem most advisable to their authors; it affords an adequate protection to the interests of remainder-men; and it supplies facilities for granting agricultural leases for a length fully sufficient to justify the occupant in laying out money on improvements, for a term, indeed, which few prudent farmers, mindful of the vicissitudes of their profession and the uncertainties of the future, would be anxious to enlarge. The Act of 1856 was however last year repealed, and another statute, entitled the Settled Estates Act, substantially repeating its provisions, enacted in its stead.* By the new act the tenant for life, who may grant agricultural leases for twenty-one years in England, is empowered to make a similar demise for no less than thirty-five years in Ireland, to take effect in possession within a year of the execution of the instrument.

It would at present be probably premature to affirm with confidence that the agricultural tenant is likely to derive material benefit from the Agricultural Holdings Act of 1875,† a measure to which the present Prime Minister attached such high importance as to prefer its safety to that

---

* St. 40 and 41. Vict. c. 18. For a full account of the provisions of the new act see Joshua Williams' *Law of Real Property*, pp. 26, 27. 12th ed.: 1877.

† St. 38 and 39. Vict. c. 92, amended by St. 39 and 40. Vict. c. 74.

of our merchant seamen. It unfortunately happens that the adoption of the provisions of the act, as is the case with so much of the legislation of the last four years, is purely optional; whence it may not be rash to conclude that, according to the opinion epigrammatically expressed by Lord Granville, while the good landlord does not require the act the bad landlord will usually contract himself out of it. In point of fact, many landlords remarkable for their liberality in their dealings with their tenants * have declined to place themselves under its operation; and such a course, as far as the writer's knowledge extends, has been very generally adopted in the case of College property, by the insertion of a simple clause in new or renewed leases, to which the lessees appear to make no objection. Under this statute, a tenant at will is entitled to compensation for improvements; but such tenancies are in practice so inconvenient to both parties as to be scarcely ever adopted even in the most strictly settled estates; and the improvements likely to be effected by tenants of this class may be generally estimated as *nil*. In the case of annual leases a year's notice, expiring with a year of tenancy, is substituted for the six months' notice formerly required. The improvements for which compensation may be claimed under the act are divided into three classes, to be considered as exhausted at the end of twenty years, seven years and two years respectively; and the landlord is empowered to charge the holding with repayment of the amount so paid over to the outgoing tenant, on condition that, unless he is absolute owner, the holding shall be freed from such incumbrance, arising by way of interest or instalments, at the period when the improvements for the purposes of the Act are regarded as exhausted. A further provision is made as to what has been often pointed out as a tenant's grievance—the law of agricultural fixtures. Where a tenant has, with the landlord's consent, affixed to the holding any engine, machinery or other fixtures for which he is not under the Act or

---

* It is stated that *every* landowning member of the present cabinet has declined to place his relations with his tenants under the operation of this valuable measure.

otherwise entitled to compensation, he is authorised to remove it on the expiration of his tenancy, subject to the landlord's option of purchasing the same.* The hardship arising from the decision as to "mere agricultural buildings" in the celebrated case of *Elwes v. Maw* may thus be considered to have been in great measure removed.

It will thus appear that the position of a farmer on a settled estate is, as the result of comparatively recent enactments, practically the same as that of the occupier under a fee-simple owner; and that the tenant for life is in all ordinary cases able to confer on his under-tenant all the stability of position necessary to encourage a liberal system of cultivation. It remains to consider the last objection indicated above, namely, that the practice of settlement has gravely diminished the facilities for the transfer of land. It is no doubt partly as an indirect result of this system that land must be regarded as a dear commodity, and one only accessible to men of capital who are prepared to purchase in considerable quantities; but on the whole there seems much reason to believe that this is not a circumstance which the economist should regret. As a matter of fact, putting aside the not inconsiderable percentage of unsettled land, the process of re-settlement is so frequently in operation and so regularly involves the sale and transfer of portions of settled estates, that land is constantly in the market; a purchaser can generally find without having long to wait the kind of estate of which he is in search; and the grievances of which he has a fair right to complain seem to arise mainly from the legal expenses of conveyance, and the cost of verifying titles, which might certainly be greatly obviated by a far less sweeping measure than the total abolition of entails.

The introduction of a bill to facilitate and simplify the transfer of land appears to be regarded as incumbent on every succeeding Chancellor; but the measures which have been hitherto passed, so far from settling the question, have plainly shewn that it is incapable of satisfactory solution

* The provisions of the act on this point are fully recounted in Williams' *Personal Property*, pp. 16, 17.

unless a general register of titles, of which the evidence shall be incontestable, or at all events a universal system of registering all deeds, whether of mortgage or conveyance, and all wills demising landed property, founded on those methods of registering now adopted in Scotland, Yorkshire and Middlesex, be compulsorily established throughout the kingdom. In such case, all grants of rent charges and others affecting control over the soil, and all deeds barring entail, now enrolled in the Chancery Division, should be collected and made easily accessible at the same place. The expenses arising from the extravagant employment of "common forms," that is, of superfluous phraseology intended merely to swell the bill of costs, are of such a nature that improvement in this respect must be looked for from the solicitors themselves, who may in time become conscious of the patent fact that more frequent transfers and less reluctant purchasers, even of smaller estates and with smaller bills of costs, would in the end become more really lucrative to the profession than the present system. This indeed is one of those matters which might be fully considered by agencies like the Incorporated Law Society, or the Annual Conference of Solicitors.

Something however has certainly been effected by the recent Acts. The Vendor and Purchaser Act of 1874,[*] which checked the habit of "tacking" by mortgagees, and which Mr. Williams speaks of as "a very objectionable enactment, in the absence of any general registry of title deeds," was repealed in the following year by the Land Transfer Act of 1875, which repeated many of its provisions.[†] This Act came into force at the beginning of last year and, it is hoped, will provide intending purchasers of land with increased facilities. By these measures a forty years' title is in ordinary cases substituted for the examination extending back for sixty years which was formerly required. Recitals, &c., twenty years old are to be considered as sufficient evidence of the facts to which they refer, subject to any express stipulation to the contrary,

---

[*] St. 37 and 38 Vict., c. 78. [†] St. 38 and 39 Vict., c. 87.

instead of, as formerly, requiring the insertion of a special stipulation to be so accepted.* The Act of 1875 also abolishes a former "Act to facilitate the Proof of Title and the conveyance of Real Estates,"† and contains new provisions with the same object. With regard to the probable effect of these provisions it may be sufficient to cite the cautious observations of Mr. Joshua Williams, in the latest edition of his Treatise on the Law of Real Property. He remarks:—

Registration under this Act is optional, and its success is too doubtful to justify any lengthened account of it in an elementary work like the present. The system of official investigation of title once for all is a good one, provided it be made by competent persons and under sufficient safeguards. . . . . If the Act should tend to an efficient system of registration of assurances throughout the kingdom it would, in the author's opinion, be the means of conferring a great benefit on the community. This however cannot be advantageously done, without resort to the printing of registered deeds and of probates of wills, and the abolition of payments by length.‡

The examination of the question of land transfer and its relation to the practice of settlement—that is, to the custom of Primogeniture which is indissolubly connected with that system—would still be incomplete, if I left altogether unnoticed one proposal for the simplication of the law which appears at the present time to be steadily growing in favour with politicians, jurists and economists alike. I refer to the proposed assimilation of the law of realty to the law of personalty. The difference between these two branches of law has generally become widely marked at a comparatively early period in the history of legal systems—at the period, in fact, when "personalty" began to have any practical value at all—whether the division has been into things

* Williams, *Real Property*. Ed. 12th, pp. 449, 450.
† St. 25 and 26 Vict., c. 53.
‡ Williams, *Real Property* Ed. 12th, p. 467. The attainment of a perfect system of registration, giving at once a sufficient guarantee both of title and extent of interest in land, is far from chimerical; see for instance reports by Dr. Hübbe, on the Hamburg Register of Land, and by Mr. Morier, on the system of conveyancing in the Grand Duchy of Hesse, among the official reports from Her Majesty's Representatives, respecting Tenure of Land, above referred to. The substance of the accounts furnished by these gentlemen is given by Mr. Fowler, *Cobden Club Essays*, pp. 180, 181.

which did or did not "require a mancipation," or, as among most modern states which have based their jurisprudence on the civil law, between moveables and immoveables. Since its first establishment, one of the main reasons why this distinction has been prized and maintained has been derived from the increased facilities which it afforded for the rapid and convenient transfer of those subjects of enjoyment and possession which, in a community not exclusively agricultural, are also the most frequent objects of sale and barter; while at a still more advanced period in the history of legal conceptions a stage seems naturally to come when public opinion demands that, either by the operation of an equitable jurisdiction or by direct legislative provisions, all classes of property shall be rendered equally accessible to the purchaser, and susceptible of conveyance from hand to hand with equal facility and freedom. The adoption of such a change as that to which I have referred has perhaps been regarded on the one hand with unnecessary forebodings of the danger, on the other with extravagant expectations of the benefit, which would thence result. The consideration of its expediency with reference to the law of intestate succession must be reserved for a separate section. It may however be here remarked that the assimilation of realty to personalty has sometimes been rashly considered as a proposition of the same character as that which would abolish the law of settlement and entail. In point of fact, the two proposals are not only very different, but are in fact irreconcilable with one another. Mr. Fowler, in his "Essay on the Land Question," has clearly recognised this circumstance, and, writing in favour of the abolition of entails, argues, somewhat inconsistently with the general current of his essay, that there is no reason to apply a similar rule to personalty, and that the latter may be left subject to settlement, as at present, while real property is taken out of the reach of such restrictions.[*] Personal property is at present quite as capable of being settled as real, though not in the same manner.[†] The aid of Chancery is to a greater extent

---

[*] Cobden Club Essays, *ut supra*, pp. 159, 160.
[†] See Joshua Williams, *Personal Property*, Part IV., ch. 1, "Of settlements of personal property."

required, and settlements can seldom have so long an effect as when they deal with land; whence it follows that, if the law of landed property were made the same, settlements would still be employed, although their nature would be somewhat different, and, their operation being more restricted, resettlement would on the whole be more frequently required. The really considerable difficulty which in the present state of the law is often encountered in distinguishing one class of property from another, a difficulty which no layman would find it easy to comprehend or to surmount,* certainly furnishes an argument for placing both on a footing of equality. Without expressing any decided opinion on this point, I may perhaps venture to conclude this section by another quotation from Mr. Joshua Williams. In the last paragraph of his work, he enunciates in the following words a view which we may assume to have been the result of a mature experience of the subject, and which certainly—coming as it does from one who is known to have devoted his life to the successful study of real property law—is deserving of the most deferential consideration :—

From what has already been said, the reader will perceive that the law of England has two different systems of rules for regulating the enjoyment and transfer of property; that the laws of real estate, though venerable for their antiquity, are in the same degree ill adapted to the requirements of modern society; whilst the laws of personal property, being of more recent origin, are proportionably suited to modern times. Over them both has arisen the jurisdiction of the Court of Chancery, by means of which the ancient strictness and simplicity of our real property laws have been in a measure rendered subservient to the arrangements and modifications of ownership, which the various necessities of society have required. Added to this have been continual enactments, especially of late years, by which many of the most glaring evils have been remedied, but by which, at the same time, the symmetry of the laws of real property has been greatly impaired. Those laws cannot indeed be now said to form a system; their present state is certainly not that in which they can remain. For the future, perhaps, the wisest course to be followed would be to aim as far as possible at a uniformity of system in the laws of both kinds of property; and, for this purpose, rather to take the laws of personal estate as the model, to which the laws of real estate should be made to conform, than on the

---

* See for instance the celebrated case of *Ackroyd* v. *Smithson*.

one hand to preserve untouched all the ancient rules, because they once were useful, or, on the other, to be annually plucking off, by parliamentary enactments, the fruit which such rules must, until eradicated necessarily produce.*

It only remains to add that the foregoing investigation of the subject appears to shew that a system of entail, unless accompanied by carefully devised securities against abuse, is likely in its consequences to be inimical to good agriculture and economically objectionable; that it would seem to be the case that in our own country, by the wisdom of Parliament and the liberality and intelligence of the great majority of landlords, the evils incident to an unrestricted practice of entailing have been really reduced to a *minimum;* that all counter-proposals appear to contain the germs of consequences even more pernicious than those which the worst conceivable method of entailing, if habitually pursued, could possibly engender; and that on the whole, looking at the condition of English agriculture in the present and its history in the past, and comparing its progress with that of other countries where different laws prevail, it is far better to maintain our own system, with such changes in detail as may be proved requisite by experience, than to run the risk of the almost certain consequences of any radical alteration in the law, or of any effective restraints on the present liberty of entailing in favour of the eldest son.†

---

* Williams, *Real Property*, p. 468.

† Montalembert, writing a quarter of a century ago of the English land-law, makes the following remark:—Tant que cette législation restera debout, tant qu'elle ne subira d'autre changement que ceux qui en restreindront les abus et en perfectionneront le maintien, on peut être rassuré sur l'avenir de l'Angleterre. L'orage ne grondera sérieusement pour elle que le jour où un mouvement d'opinion se déclarera contre les substitutions. Alors, mais alors seulement, elle fera le premier pas sur cette pente qui précipite les peuples, à travers les secousses des révolutions, dans les bas-fonds du despotisme. *De l'avenir politique de l'Angleterre:* ch. vii. *De la liberté de tester*, pp. 115, 116. 3me Ed.

SECTION V.—SOCIAL AND POLITICAL ASPECTS OF PRIMOGENITURE.

THE social and domestic effects of Primogeniture, and the political aspects of the same institution, are so important in themselves, and so intimately connected with its economical import, that no apology perhaps is requisite for devoting to this branch of the subject a few pages of discussion. Let us first consider the matter from the point of view of the domestic forum, and briefly analyse some of the objections which have been brought against the custom as prejudicial to the true interests and proper relations of the father, the eldest son, and the younger children.

It is said, in the first place, that the present law has a tendency to place the father in a false position, and one which it is unseemly for a parent to occupy. When, as is often the case, on a son's attaining his majority it is thought desirable to re-settle an estate, it sometimes happens that the father has incurred debts, arising perhaps from expenditure on improvements, perhaps from rash speculation or some even less creditable cause, possibly from circumstances beyond his own control, which he is anxious to take the opportunity of charging on the estate, or meeting by a sale of a portion of the property. Possibly he may wish to marry again, and is desirous to provide a jointure for a second wife, or to acquire facilities for creating portions for possible children. Under such circumstances, it is said that the practical decision rests with the son, who is called in to judge his father's actions, to condone his former imprudence, or sanction his matrimonial projects. As a matter of fact, however, there is every reason to believe that family settlements are usually arranged on a basis of generosity and mutual good feeling; the son often has at least as much as the father to gain by the instrument in the execution of which he participates; and when it is remembered how much misery and distress is caused to others by any reckless extravagance or culpable neglect on the part of the possessor of a large estate, we may well believe that the consciousness that he will be expected at no distant period to give some account of his stewardship, exercises on the whole a wholesome influence as a restraint upon such misconduct. The custom of settlement would not be so popular among our aristocracy were it habitually attended by such disagreeable incidents as certain ingenious writers have succeeded in evolving out of their inner consciousness. It is a sound maxim, though one often misapplied, that "hard cases make bad law;" and we can scarcely be expected to remodel the whole system of entailing because it may have the effect of embittering the family relations in a few exceptional instances.

It is not so easy to deny that the law of Primogeniture not unfrequently exercises an ill effect on the persons who are popularly supposed alone to benefit by it—the heirs of landed proprietors. If naturally indolent, they are apt to arrive at the conclusion that there is no special need for them to exert themselves; and if disposed to extravagance they often find it easy to raise money on the security of their expectations. The supposition that they enjoy very exceptional facilities in this respect is however to a great extent erroneous. The son of a rich merchant or manufacturer, who does not own an acre of settled land, finds the money-lenders very nearly as accommodating as they prove to the heir of a large entailed estate. In the latter case, they have the security of a *post-obit*, which may not be realised for many years; in the former they trust, with a confidence justified by experience, that a feeling of honour, or the desire to avoid a scandal, on the part of father or son, will ensure the satisfaction of a percentage of their exorbitant claims sufficiently large to make their trade remunerative. It is said, moreover, that the eldest son, conscious that his father's displeasure cannot affect his expectations, is apt to shew himself deficient in filial duty; while the younger children are supposed to feel a natural jealousy of his exclusive advantages. It can only be replied that these theories seem to have no very substantial foundation in experience, by the light of which alone their validity can be judged. On such a matter it is of course impossible to produce statistics, or pronounce a very dogmatic opinion; but it is not difficult to shew that any other system might with equal facility be attacked as producing equally pernicious effects on domestic happiness and the authority of parents. If the existing law were superseded by one of compulsory partition, under which the parent was bound to leave the bulk of his fortune, irrespective of his inclinations, in equal portions to all his children, the undutifulness and indifference to the father's wishes which is now, on very little evidence, attributed to eldest sons might, on not less cogent grounds, be attributed to all the sons alike. In neither case, in the opinion of the present writer, would such gloomy anticipations be frequently realised in fact, for the simple reason that family affection and filial obedience are not entirely or even principally engendered by pecuniary considerations, or that enlightened calculation of self-interest which the utilitarian philosopher regards as the only reasonable source of human action. Once more, if the father were allowed to dispose of his real estate, in all cases, exactly as he pleased, if the law contented itself with abolishing the exceptional privileges of the eldest son without introducing any scheme of compulsory equality in their stead, it might plausibly be argued that, instead of one son being indolent and extravagant and the rest jealous and discontented, all would alike exhibit the not less objectionable traits of mutual suspicion, and would endeavour, by artifice and intrigue, to supersede one another in the parental affection. But all such theories are really vitiated by the unnecessarily sordid view of human nature which they involve. Those who know anything of the feelings commonly entertained towards each other by the members of a large middle-class family, where the father's property consists of personalty alone, will at once recognise the absurdity of such a picture; but it is no further removed from the truth than some of the imaginary evils of Primogeniture of which we hear so much. Neither does it appear that an extension of the liberty of bequest, any more than a law of *légitime*, would perceptibly or necessarily increase the dutifulness, obedience or filial reverence of children, virtues which, as suggested above, spring from very different causes than the hope of a precarious gain in the distant future. It is somewhat remarkable that while America is the land in which the children are most entirely dependent on the pleasure or caprice of the parent, and where the dispositions of the latter are unchecked, to an extent elsewhere unknown, either by law or public opinion, it is also in America that we observe the independence of children, at an early age, pushed to the greatest extreme. The fact is that, as De Tocqueville long since remarked, the influence of the father is always much greater in an aristocracy than a democracy; it is therefore greatest in a country where the law of Primogeniture, the mainstay of an aristocracy, exists. "Du moment," he writes, "où le jeune Américain s'approche de la virilité, les liens d'obeissance filiale se détendent de jour en jour. Maître de ses pensées, il l'est bientôt après de sa conduite . . . la division des patrimoines qu'amène la démocratie contribue peut être plus que tout le reste à changer les rapports du père et des enfants . . . ainsi dans le même temps que le pouvoir échappe a l'aristocratie, on voit disparaître ce qu'il y avait d'austére, de conventionnel, et de légal dans la puissance paternelle et un sort d'égalité s'établit autour du foyer domestique . . . dans la famille démocratique le père n'exerce guère d'autre pouvoir que celui qu'on se plaît à accorder à la tendresse et à l'expérience d'un vieillard."* In the face of these conclusions and observations as to the effect on the domestic relations of a system either of compulsory partition or unrestrained liberty of bequest, we are perhaps entitled to inquire of those who on this ground assail the custom of Primogeniture, what rule more efficacious in securing the attainment of an end to which they rightly attach so high a value they are prepared to promulgate in its place?

De Tocqueville also calls attention in an interesting note to the circumstance that while the public or political institu-

---

* *De la Démocratie en Amérique*, Vol. IV, pp. 60, 64, 65, 66.

tions of America are much more democratic than those of France, the civil legislation, as illustrated by the absence of any law of equal succession, is far less so. He attributes this phenomenon to the circumstance that the author of the *code civile* was unwilling, as many of his acts attest—and notably his unsuccessful efforts to establish a new aristocracy in the place of the old *noblesse*—to extend the democratic principle beyond the sphere of the private relations of the citizens to that of the constitutional polity. The influence of the former on the latter is, however, so constant in its pressure and overwhelming in its force, that it is certain ultimately to prevail against all artificial barriers or dynastic cunning. As our author observes of Napoleon, "Tandis que le torrent démocratique déborderait sur les lois civiles, il ésperait se tenir aisément à l'abri derrière les lois politiques. Cette vue était à la fois pleine d'habilété et d'égoisme; mais un pareil compromis ne pouvait être durable. Car, à la longue, la société politique ne saurait manquer de devenir l'expression et l'image de la société civile; et c'est dans ce sens qu'on peut dire qu'il n'y a rien de plus politique chez un peuple que la législation civile."[*]

I return to the more immediate consideration of Primogeniture in its domestic aspects, and especially in its bearing on the position of that class so frequently depicted as deserving objects of public commiseration—the younger sons of landed proprietors. The system of equal division, writes Blackstone, "has the appearance of the greatest impartiality and justice, at least in the opinion of younger brothers;"[†] while others have asserted that the equity of the custom of Primogeniture has been seldom recognised except by eldest sons. In point of fact, an *argumentum ad hominem* of this kind is altogether inappropriate; and it might perhaps be shewn that those who have on various occasions most vigorously assailed or most energetically supported the present law have been precisely those with the smallest personal interest in its operation or effects. It is sometimes urged that Primogeniture deprives the younger children of their legitimate

[*] *De la Démocratie,* &c., Vol. IV., pp. 61, 62, note.
[†] 2 Blackstone Com., 215.

rights; but such an argument certainly seems to imply some confusion of thought on the part of those who use it. It would appear to be a sufficiently obvious proposition that a man's right to property, whether legal or moral, must arise either from his having acquired it by his own exertions, or from the conduct of others having implanted in his mind a reasonable expectation that he would succeed to it. Now the position of a younger son satisfies neither of these conditions; he certainly did not acquire the paternal estate, and from his earliest years he has been aware that in all probability it will devolve upon another. Complaints of the injustice of Primogeniture are indeed seldom heard from the lips of those to whom it is supposed to be unjust. The cadet of an ancestral family, on the contrary, starts in life with many advantages which he mainly owes to the existence of that law. He generally enjoys an annuity which, though insignificant in comparison with the nominal fortune indicated by the rent-roll of his elder brother, and not so ample as to leave him with no stimulus to independent exertion, is yet sufficient to give him a start in life, which many of his less fortunate rivals have cause to envy. In a word, he is neither "cursed with a competence," nor crippled by the necessity of earning his entire livelihood. Moreover, the influence of the family name, the family connections, and the family wealth is actively exercised on his behalf. In the paternal mansion he is always a welcome guest; among the neighbouring gentry, he is received with the consideration which his birth demands. In the professions, or the service of the Crown, his path is to a great extent made smooth for him; the merits of a deserving scion of the landed aristocracy are rapidly recognised; and he has special opportunities of adding to his fortune by a judicious marriage with a member of some wealthy family, willing by such an alliance to unite recently acquired riches with ancestral rank. There is indeed scarcely any position in the State to which such an one, if blest with good abilities, may not reasonably aspire; while, if nature has not endowed him with mental gifts, the credit of his family demands that some kind of honourable career shall be invented for his behoof.*

One indirect consequence of the English law deserves particular attention. We have in this country hereditary noblemen; but we possess no order of nobility. This circumstance is in itself sufficient to explain the different degree of consideration attached to a British peer, and a member, for instance, of the French *noblesse*, or a Russian Prince. The absence among ourselves of a noble class is no doubt susceptible of historical explanation. It in part arose from the manner in which the Thegns, who supplanted the older Eorls, were first created. Thegnhood was in fact a nobility of office bestowed by the King; and on the death of the office-holder, the office itself became vacant. A custom soon arose by which the eldest son succeeded to his father's place in the counsels of the throne; but the multiplication of such places, so as to make room for all of noble birth, was of course impossible. Thus it happened that the younger sons and descendants of a peer necessarily remained undistinguished, except perhaps by courtesy, from the commons of the realm. This is in substance the explanation which Mr. Freeman, who in more than one passage emphatically directs attention to the fact that in England there is no noble class, himself gives of the difference between our own system and that of Germany or France; and his language is worth quoting, although it might be wished that he had brought into greater prominence the circumstance that our own institution could not possibly have been maintained without that strict application of the doctrine of Primogeniture which has always been so eminently characteristic of English law and custom:—

"What was it," he asks, "that hindered the nobility thus formed

* Toutefois, on aurait tort de croire que, chez les peuples aristocratiques, les privilèges de l'aîné ne fussent avantageux qu'à lui seul, et qu'ils n'excitassent autour de lui que l'énvie et la haine. L'aîné s'efforce d'ordinaire de procurer la richesse et le pouvoir à ses frères, parce que l'éclat général de la maison rejaillit sur celui qui la représente; et les cadets cherchent à faciliter à l'aîné toutes ses enterprises, parce que la grandeur et la force du chef de la famille le met de plus en plus en état d'en élever tous les rejetons.—De Tocqueville, *ut supra*, Vol. IV., p. 67.

from becoming a real nobility? What saved us from a *noblesse* or *Adel* in the foreign sense? For I repeat that in England we have, in strictness, no nobility; we have no class which keeps on, from generation to generation, in the possession of exclusive privileges, either political or social. Our peerage is not a nobility in the sense in which nobility is understood in foreign lands. It is not only a rank to which any man may rise, but it is a rank from which the descendants of the hereditary holders must as a matter of course come down. Political privilege belongs only to one member of a family at a time; honorary precedence does not go beyond one or two generations. This is not nobility in the sense which that word bears in those lands where all the descendants of a noble are noble for ever. Why then did not the Thegnhood of England grow into a nobility such as that which in other lands grew out of the same elements? . . . That great law of William which made every man in the land the man of the king had much to do with it; but, paradoxical as it may sound, I conceive that the very power and dignity of the peerage has had a good deal to do with it also. Elsewhere nobility was primarily a matter of rank and privilege, with which political power might or might not be connected. But in an English peerage the primary idea is political power; rank and privilege are a mere adjunct. The peer does not hold a mere rank which he can share with his descendants; he holds an office, which passes to his next heir when he dies, but which he cannot share with any man while he lives. The peer then, not a mere noble, but a legislator, a counsellor, and a judge,[*] holds a distinct place in the State, which his children can no more share with him than anyone else. Hence in England we have but two classes, Peers and Commoners, those who hold the office and authority of a peer and those who do not. The children of a peer come under this last head as much as other men; they are therefore Commoners. The very existence of the peerage of itself hinders the existence of a nobility in the true sense of the word."[†]

The existence in England of this state of things, thus lucidly enunciated and historically explained by Mr. Freeman, as contrasted with the system of hereditary nobility prevalent upon the Continent, appears to the present writer to be, both socially and politically, of almost unmixed advantage. It is one of the results, and certainly not the least important result, of the law and custom of Primogeniture. With us the eldest son of the Baron becomes himself eventually a Baron also; but his younger son only receives by courtesy the designation of "Honourable;" and none of the children

[*] The judicial powers of the House of Lords have by recent legislation been nominally retained and practically abolished.
[†] Freeman, E. A., *Comparative Politics*, pp. 263-265.

of the latter enjoy any sort of titular recognition or are distinguished, otherwise than by their family name, from the most vulgar *parvenu* of yesterday. A constant mingling of classes is thus effected; the influences of birth and culture permeate downwards and are widely diffused; and the maxim of "*noblesse oblige,*" if not ostentatiously professed, is tacitly recognised as a guide to conduct by many who are only noble through an amiable though illogical confusion of thought. If the bearer of a famous name commits an unbecoming action he is thought to have disgraced others besides himself; and the consciousness of their descent must often exercise a wholesome influence on many an obscure, perhaps doubtful, scion of the house of Bedford, of Norfolk, or of Argyll. Neither is this the only or the chief benefit which we derive from the constitution of our peerage. The peerage is an elastic and changing body to which, while some are constantly descending from it, others as frequently ascend. The owner of splendid wealth and large estates may reasonably hope to be called to the counsels of his sovereign, and to found a new line of legislators and peers; the performer of eminent public services is entitled to look for the same reward; a patent of nobility frequently crowns a distinguished career in diplomacy; every briefless barrister is a potential Chancellor, and every new-fledged curate is potentially a spiritual peer. If we wish to fully appreciate the benefits which we derive from this constant intermingling of classes, and translation of individuals from one class to another, it will be enough to cast a momentary glance at some of the effects of the more rigid system which generally prevails on the Continent—in France, for example, or in Russia.

The sign of nobility in France is the prefix *de* before the surname; and the possession of this prefix, though without political significance, is of great social importance. The bearer of it is always regarded as a person of consideration; he who lacks it is considered a nobody. There are at the present day in republican and democratic France three distinct classes, *la noblesse, la bourgeoisie,* and *le peuple,* separated from each other by a wide line of demarcation; and what is called society consists entirely of those who are ranked under the first of these heads. At the time of marriage, it becomes of immense importance to a Frenchman whether he does or does not possess the *de*. In the former case, however reduced his fortune, he can reckon on improving it by a wealthy alliance with some *bourgeoise* family; in the latter no such opportunities will be open to him, while he will seldom find it possible to persuade a lady—or rather the parents of a lady—of gentle birth, even if in impoverished circumstances, to give her hand to a plebeian. Many curious instances of the influence on matrimonial projects of this, to a stranger, insignificant prefix are given by Mr. Hamerton, in his interesting work on Rural Life in France; and they certainly go far to prove that the spirit of romance is not, as we are sometimes told, altogether extinct among our neighbours across the Channel.*

It is perhaps only a natural consequence of the artificial value set upon the *de* that it is often falsely assumed by persons who have not the slightest claim to use it. The nobility having no political privileges, there is little in the law to check such a practice; while by the discreet use of cautious and gradual methods the condonation of public opinion can often be obtained. A man, for instance, buys some small estate; and proceeds after signing his name to add, at first in brackets, that of his property, merely of course in order to distinguish himself from other persons having the same surname. The brackets however are soon removed; the old plebeian name then completely disappears; and M. Machin, who has made a fortune by his *usines*, who, for convenience sake, on becoming a rural proprietor, styled himself Machin (de Roulongeau), who a few years afterwards was known as Machin de Roulongeau, in the end developes into Monsieur de Roulongeau, the lineal representative forsooth of the ancient barons of that line.† *Il n'y a que le premier pas qui coûte.* The false title is sure to be consecrated by time; and no government can venture to expose

---

* *Round my House*, pp. 88-91.   † *Ibid.*

such assumptions for fear of injuring its own friends. The Legitimists would be thought most inclined to take some such step; but it is said that the most ardent Legitimists are to be found among the fictitious nobility. Such persons are sure to be what is called *bien pensant;* it belongs to the character they assume; and it would not be very rash to conjecture that the most energetic supporters of the revolutionary government of Marshal MacMahon, which impertinently claimed the title of "Conservative," were to be found among those who, like the vulgar Minister of the Interior himself, had falsely arrogated the prefix *de* to their own names. If this fiction once receives official recognition it becomes a fact; and when the government wishes to enlist the support of an individual like M. Machin it will generally shew little hesitation in inserting his assumed title in some official document, which at once stamps it as genuine.

Contemptible as these practices may seem, it is by no means clear that we have not been ourselves saved from something of the same kind, not so much by any special insular exemption from the failing of "snobbishness," as by the circumstances adverted to above. If there were in this country an order of nobility, and every person outside its ranks were regarded as of vulgar character and low extraction, and if there were no legitimate means of gaining a footing among the titled class, it is quite likely that we should witness equally despicable attempts to effect an illegitimate entry. Mr. Hamerton seasonably reminds those who would assume an air of virtuous indignation, how common among ourselves is the false assumption of the heraldic emblems of ancient families by persons who are well aware that they are acting without the slightest colour of right; while others, not satisfied with the names their fathers bore, transform themselves into Howards or Seymours by means of an advertisement in *The Times.*

If we turn to Russia, we shall find that the existence of a patrician caste has not there generated precisely similar evils; but at the same time the results can scarcely be regarded as satisfactory. Nobility is not sought by fair means or foul, for the simple reason that nobility in itself has lost all its value. All the sons of a Prince are themselves Princes; and the statement that in Russia you meet with whole villages of "Princes" is scarcely an exaggeration. The result is that in Russia there are no distinctions save those which flow from autocratic favour; birth counts for absolutely nothing; official rank, rank in the service of the State, or the confidence of the Tsar, furnish the only claims to consideration. Thus Mr. Wallace goes on to say, after describing a Prince of the highest class, one of distinguished official position at St. Petersburg, who had spent the greater part of his life in administrative work, and held a seat in the Council of State :—

"The Prince belongs to the highest rank of the Russian Noblesse. If we wish to get an idea of the lowest rank, we have merely to go to the neighbouring village. There we shall find a number of poor, uneducated men, who live in small, squalid houses, and are not easily to be distinguished from peasants. They are nobles, like the Prince; but, unlike him, they have neither official rank nor large fortune, and their landed property consists of a few acres of poor land, which barely supplies them with the first necessaries of life. If we went to other parts of the country, we might find men in this condition bearing the title of prince! *This is the natural result of the Russian law of inheritance, which does not recognise the principle of Primogeniture with regard to titles and estates.* All the sons of a prince are princes, and *at his death his property, movable and immovable, is divided equally amongst them all.*"*

On the subject of Primogeniture, we read in the volume of Land Tenure Reports already cited :—

"There is no general law of primogeniture, although in a few great families estates have been entailed under a special law passed in the reign of the Emperor Nicholas. In 1713, Peter the Great intended to introduce a general inheritance in fee of the eldest son, but this was so much opposed to the spirit of the Russian landowners that one of the first acts of Peter II. was to cancel the ukase of 1713."†

It is difficult to avoid concluding that the Russian nobles would have consulted better for their own ultimate interests, and the stability of their position and influence in the

* Russia: by D. Mackenzie Wallace. Vol. I., p. 410. The italics are my own.
† Land Tenure Reports, Part II., p. 68.

country, had they acquiesced in the decree of their sagacious monarch. In another passage, Mr. Wallace remarks:—

"We find plenty of Russians who are proud of their wealth, of their culture, or of their official position, but we scarcely ever find a Russian who is proud of his birth or imagines that the fact of his having a long pedigree gives him any right to political privileges or to social consideration. Such ideas appear to the ordinary Russian noble absurd and ridiculous. Hence there is a certain amount of truth in the oft-repeated saying that there is in reality no aristocracy in Russia. Certainly the Noblesse as a whole cannot be called an aristocracy. If the term is to be used at all, it must be applied to a group of families which cluster around the Court and form the highest ranks of the Noblesse. This social aristocracy contains many old families, but its real basis is official rank and general culture, rather than pedigree or blood. . . . . . Though it has no peculiar privileges, its actual position in the Administration and at Court gives its members great facilities for advancement in the public service. On the other hand, its semi-bureaucratic character, *together with the law and custom of divsding landed property among the children at the death of their parents, deprives it of stability*. New men force their way into it by official distinction, whilst many of the old families are compelled by poverty to retire from its ranks. The son of a small proprietor or even of a parish priest may rise to the highest offices of State, whilst the descendants of the half-mythical Rurik may descend to the rank of peasants. It is said that not long ago a certain Prince Krapotkin gained his living as a cabman in St. Petersburg."*

It would be superfluous to dilate on the small significance attached, even in their own countries, to the title of a German Baron or an Italian Count. In whatever country there has existed a noble caste, the same results present themselves. The nobility have either lost all consideration, as such, or, shorn of political privilege, have had the mortification of seeing their titles usurped by opulent *parvenus*, eager thus to gain the *entrée* of society. The very different

* Russia, Vol. I., pp. 431, 432. According to the latest statistics, the number of hereditary nobles in Russia is 652,000 : of "personal" nobles, 374,000. With Mr. Wallace's remarks on the Russian nobility we may compare an epigrammatic sentence in which Balzac describes the effect of the revolutionary legislation on the nobility in France:—Sous la restauration, la noblesse s'est toujours souvenue d'avoir été battue et volée ; ainsi mettant à part deux ou trois exceptions, est elle devenue économe, sage, prévoyante, enfin bourgeoise et sans grandeur. Depuis, 1830 a consommé l'œuvre de 1793. En France, désormais, on aura de grands noms, mais plus de grandes maisons, à moins de changements politiques difficiles à prévoir. *Tout y prend le cachet de la personnalité. La fortune des plus sages est viagère; on y a détruit la famille.*

fortune of our own hereditary peerage is one of the fruits of the law of Primogeniture and the practice of entailing; and if that practice be abolished it is difficult to see how that fortune and position which is essential to the dignity of a peer, and without which it is impossible for him to discharge efficiently his political duties, can by possibility be maintained. Mr. Brodrick and Mr. Fowler argue strongly for giving every father an unlimited power of disinheriting an unworthy son.* Doubtless, an estate might often benefit if such an one, who had plainly shewn his incompetence, were set aside in favour of another and more deserving member of the family; but it is obvious that titles could not thus be shifted at the discretion, possibly at the caprice, of a private individual. It may moreover be hoped, and the hope would be justified by frequent experience, that one who while heir-apparent has shewn little ability or merit, will often be roused, on acceding to a large estate and an illustrious name, to an effort to discharge with credit the duties of his high position. Mr. Brodrick argues that if his proposal were adopted " since he "—the eldest son—" would depend, like his younger brothers, upon his father's award, he would, like them, betake himself to some profession or business, and endeavour to increase, instead of diminishing, his future patrimony." It would be easy to shew the incongruity which this suggestion would in many cases involve. Is the Marquis of Blandford, for instance, expected to go to the bar and support a family at Nisi Prius with a precarious hope of some day succeeding to an establishment at Blenheim? Is the Marquis of Hartington to eke out in opposition the salary which he has drawn in the past, or hopes to draw in the future, as a cabinet minister, and see Chatsworth pass into other hands? Or shall the Marquis of Stafford join the bulls and bears of the Stock Exchange, and learn on the demise of the Duke of Sutherland that Stafford House and a few hundred thousand acres with it have been bequeathed to the Hospital for Incurables, or some other beneficent institution? Mr. Brodrick demands what would be indeed

* See especially Cobden Club Essays, pp. 110-115.

a vast and sweeping change in the law; but he scarcely seems to realise that before such a change can be brought about it will be necessary to effect an alteration certainly not less vast both in public opinion and in the private feelings of the upper classes. Mr. Fowler, it is true, discusses this point in a more rational manner, and admits that it might be necessary to leave the law as it stands in the case of the peerage, while abolishing its operation over the estates of commoners;[*] but so illogical a compromise could scarcely be of permanent duration, or prove satisfactory to either class.

It would however be wrong to ignore the fact that the hereditary peerage itself is an institution not universally approved, and of which it is impossible to assert that it may not be considerably modified in the future. This is not the place in which to defend or attack the first estate; from our present point of view it is sufficient to observe that it is not so much the descent of hereditary titles, as the legislative powers attached to them, which furnish ground for hostile criticism. Those who would substitute an elective assembly for the House of Lords would still leave the deposed peers their patents of nobility, and the custom of primogeniture would still be necessary to maintain such dignity and influence as might remain attached to the class. It may however well be doubted whether such a class, if divested at once of responsibility and power, would as a class be any longer worth preserving. "Il n'y a rien," writes De Tocqueville, " de plus misérablement corrompu qu'une aristocratie qui conserve ses richesses en perdant son pouvoir et qui, reduite à des jouissances vulgaires, possède encore d'immenses loisirs. Les passions énergiques et les grandes pensées qui l'avaient animée jadis, en disparaissent alors, et l'on n'y rencontre plus guère qu'une multitude de petits vices rongeurs, qui s'attachent à elle, comme des vers à un cadavre."[†] All experience corroborates this remark. If primogeniture were devoted to the maintenance of a wealthy and unprivileged class, without political power and devoid

[*] Cobden Club Essays, pp. 147-149.
[†] De la Démocratie, &c., Vol. IV. p. 94.

of all conception of social duties correlative to their rights, it would probably work more harm than good; and the argument on its behalf, derived from its utility as an instrument for keeping together the landed property of peers of the realm, would, it may be conceded, at once fall to the ground on the abolition of the hereditary branch of the legislature.

There are however other and not less weighty pleas in its favour, which a consideration of the political aspects of Primogeniture suggests, and which would remain unaffected by such a measure. There is no branch of our administrative institutions to which a thoughtful Englishman deservedly attaches higher value than our system of local self-government. It may be unsatisfactory in some of the detailed and occasional results of its operation; its organisation is confessedly imperfect; the method in which those who manage it are chosen is undoubtedly capricious; like most other parts of our constitution it has its weaknesses, its anomalies, its failures; but when we observe the prejudicial effects of excessive bureaucracy and centralisation on the Continent, and the obstacles which they oppose to political liberty and the independent initiative of the intelligent individual, we may indeed feel grateful for the able and enlightened management of local affairs by local bodies which we ourselves enjoy. The people of England have thus acquired the habit of doing for themselves a thousand things, indispensable to health, to order, and to progress in civilisation, which the inhabitants of other countries instinctively look to the State to effect on their behalf. It has been often observed that there is no better training for the House of Commons than regular attendance at Quarter Sessions; and if the work of local administration be neglected or perfunctorily performed, it is certainly impossible to look for any genuine vitality in representative institutions. The comparative credit and success with which bodies like County Boards, Chambers of Agriculture, and the unpaid magistracy—an institution, I believe, without a parallel in the world—discharge their various functions, actuated by no hope either of pecuniary gain or public recognition, is mainly due to the existence in every county of a considerable number of large landed proprietors, endowed with sufficient leisure and sufficient wealth to devote their energies ungrudgingly to such work, and who feel that their stake in the country is such as to make it both their interest and their duty that it be accomplished in the most satisfactory manner. The practical failure, described by Mr. Wallace, of all attempts to create a satisfactory system of local administration in Russia must be mainly ascribed to the absence in that country of such a class. In France, the excessive power of the officials, too often abused for the most pernicious ends, is in great measure due to a similar cause; and indeed it is not very easy to see how, except by some law analogous to our own custom of Primogeniture, an order of independent gentlemen, indifferent to the favour or displeasure of political factions, can possibly be created or maintained.

The social value of such a class in diffusing, directly or indirectly, consciously or unconsciously, an atmosphere of refined feeling and liberal culture throughout the country is scarcely less considerable. The hereditary peer, or tenant of a great ancestral property, may perhaps have received no great amount of what is commonly known as education; but he seldom remains altogether unaffected by the educating influences among which he has always lived. He grasps intuitively those chivalrous and elevated ideas and modes of thought which others, less fortunate in their birth, only attain by a slow and laborious process of reason and reflection. If himself, by some rare accident, illiterate and coarse, the members of his family will probably exhibit a different and a purer taste; and the refining influence of the country house, with its splendid picture gallery, its noble heirlooms, its well-furnished library, its varied collection of objects of *vertu* and artistic treasures, is by some imperceptible process diffused far beyond the circle of its immediate inmates. We may indeed conclude that there are very few, even among younger sons, who, if they dispassionately weighed the benefits derived by one generation after another from such associations, would not hesitate to sacrifice them in exchange for some pecuniary gain of doubtful value, in which it would rarely happen that more than a single generation would participate. If the law were different, the ancient demesne would be sold and the paternal estate partitioned, since the plan sometimes adopted by old French families of avoiding these evils by uniting their several branches, and leading a sort of common life in the ancestral *chateau*, would be altogether uncongenial to English feeling. The younger sons would perhaps receive two-thousand a year instead of five-hundred as their portion; but they would lose the chief incentive to exertion; their own children would probably be no better off than if their parents had started in life with humbler means; while the prestige of the family name and the advantage of its influence would be irreparably lost to all its subsequent descendants. While the present system endures, we may justly apply to the family tree of an ancient house the description which the Sibyl gave of that mystic branch which, dedicated to the nether Juno, grew amid meaner foliage on the sombre slopes of pathless Avernus :—

Primo avolso non deficit alter
aureus, et simili frondescit virga metallo.

The ore is indeed of gold, and precious; and it boasts such magic spell as to refine by its unfelt touch and tacit presence the less pure metal of newer wealth which, brought into contact with it and dwelling by its side, acquires in the process of years a measure of its purity and virtue.

SECTION VI.—THE LAW OF INTESTATE SUCCESSION.

I HAVE not as yet directly adverted to the distinction between what is known as the custom, and what is rightly termed the law, of Primogeniture, a distinction sufficiently familiar to all students of the English law of property. To put the matter concisely, by the custom of Primogeniture is meant the practice of entailing land on the eldest son born of the anticipated marriage of some living person, in such a manner that, should he survive his father, it will be impossible to prevent such son from succeeding to the inheritance. The law of Primogeniture, in the stricter sense of the former word, is the rule by which, on an individual dying intestate, all his real estate devolves on his eldest son or heir-at-law, as determined by the canons of descent. The question is sometimes asked by persons of sufficient intelligence to appreciate this important difference, but not sufficiently instructed in legal history to be aware of the origin of either the law or the custom, whether the former produced the latter or the reverse process in fact occurred, in other words, whether the law was the effect of the custom or the cause of its development? Enough has been said in a preceding section to shew that to attribute either the law to the custom or the latter to the law would be historically incorrect; but that the former explanation would be the less misleading of the two. To an uncertain but very limited extent the existing law may be said to influence the existing custom; but both are based on a much older law which left no scope for individual choice. We have seen that, not long after the Norman Conquest, the right of the eldest son to inherit his father's land, at first in theory a mere customary succession dependent on the donor's pleasure became, in the case of lands held by knight's service, an indefeasible prerogative, a prerogative of which he could not be divested either by lord or tenant; that the latter gradually acquired the right of alienating during his life-time, but seldom, and only for certain special purposes, exercised that right to the detriment of his heir; that by a judicial decision, in the reign of the fourth Edward, the father acquired full power, whatever his estate, to disinherit his son by a collusive action; that by the Statute of Wills, passed under Henry the Eighth, the right of testamentary bequest was partially conceded; and that by an incidental effect of the abolition of feudal tenures on the Restoration that right, previously limited in its exercise, was extended to the whole estate.

At the same time, after the full liberty of alienating during life-time had been recognised by law, the force of custom and the inclinations of parents contributed in most cases to preserve the ancient method of descent; and the invention in the seventeenth century of the modern system of settlements to a great extent secured such devolution, and once more withdrew it from the control of each succeeding tenant. Similarly, after a plenary right of testamentary disposition had been granted to landowners, many who had not otherwise disposed of their property, declined to avail themselves of this method of doing so; and the law naturally presumed that such persons were acquainted with its provisions, and wished their estates to descend intact to the normal heir. Hence it happens that all realty still devolves, on a parent dying intestate, on the eldest male descendant of the eldest line.*

The case of personal property has long been recognised by the law as very different, and requiring different rules for its distribution on intestacy. It does not indeed very frequently happen that the owner of a considerable real estate, of which he is free to dispose as he pleases, dies without making a will or prescribing its devolution by some other means; and when such is the case the omission is often the result of deliberate purpose. Moreover, as we

---

* It would be superfluous to here explain the precise effect of the technical rules by which, since the act for the amendment of the law of inheritance, the descent of realty is governed. The main points are, (1) The heir is traced from the last *purchaser*, a word which in legal phraseology bears a special sense,; (2) males are preferred to females; (3) when two or more males are of the same degree of consanguinity the eldest is preferred; and (4) the lineal descendants *in infinitum* of a deceased person represent their ancestor.

learn from the Parliamentary Return of 1875, the number of landowners in the kingdom, including those whose freehold is of the smallest dimensions, and many who only possess "terms of years" which are not technically real property at all, is less than a million; while most adults possess on their decease some personal property to dispose of, which is often however so small in amount that it never occurs to them to incur the anxiety or the expense involved in making a will. Many too who earn considerable incomes, and are seldom without a substantial balance at their bankers, die intestate in middle life. They have perhaps never given the subject any consideration; more probably they have simply postponed what it is felt can be done at any time to some less busy season; and they often justify themselves in doing so on the ground that they are on the whole satisfied with the prospect of their property being administered by their relatives according to the provisions of the law.

On the death of an intestate, administration of his or her property is granted, usually to the widow, widower, or next of kin, on application to the Probate Division of the High Court of Justice. The administrator then divides the effects in accordance with the provisions of two enactments, passed in the reigns of Charles the Second and James the Second, and known by the name of the Statutes of Distribution.* These Statutes appear to have for the first time accurately defined the respective rights of the various relatives of the deceased, and the method of distribution which they prescribe must be regarded as on the whole of a satisfactory and equitable kind. In accordance with these enactments, if the intestative leave children but no widow the whole, if both children and a widow, two-thirds of his personal estate, after the claims of creditors have beeen satisfied, are divided among the former in equal shares. If he also leaves real estate the heir is still entitled to his share in the personal property; he could indeed until within the present reign, as has been already mentioned, claim to have mortgage

* St. 22 and 23 Car. II. c. 10 : and St. 1 Jac. II. c. 17.

debts and other incumbrances charged on the land first satisfied out of the personalty, like ordinary debts, before the apportionment of the residue amongst the next of kin. If the intestate leave a widow and no children, the former is entitled to a half instead of a third of his assets, the remaining half going to his father, or, if the latter be dead, his mother, brothers and sisters in equal shares; while if there be neither widow nor children, the father, if there be neither widow, children nor father, the mother, brothers and sisters, and if there be none of these relatives, nor children of the latter, the next of kin, traced according to the rules of the civil law, succeed in equal shares to the personal estate.*

This method of distribution appears to afford general satisfaction, and to require little if any amendment. Certainly none would advocate the descent of personal like real property to the heir-at-law; but of late years a proposal to assimilate the law of intestate succession to realty to that of personalty has been received with much and, as far as can be judged, increasing favour. There is indeed much to be said for such a change; and indeed one of the arguments most frequently employed in defence of the present law is that, for reasons already adverted to, its practical effects are extremely insignificant. If however a law is in itself a bad one the assertion that it is seldom allowed to operate can scarcely be regarded as a sufficient excuse for its retention. It may willingly be conceded that the direct effects on the tenure of land which a change in the law in this direction would produce would be relatively inconsiderable; although the assertion, which has been made on several occasions, that not more than two per cent. of the realty in the country descends by the rules of intestate succession, is probably below the mark. One remark, however, must here be made. It is scarcely fair for those who support the existing law to defend it simultaneously on two contrary grounds. At one moment, we are told that the law is too unimportant to be worth the trouble of reforming; while the next argument we hear is

* For a full explanation of the rules here roughly sketched, see Joshua Williams' *Personal Property* pp. 396-399. Ninth Edition.

that the custom of Primogeniture is inseparably bound up with the present law of intestacy. It was apparently for this latter reason that the Real Property Commissioners, appointed in 1828, reported in favour of the devolution of an intestate's realty to his heir, as being " far better adapted to the constitution and habits of this kingdom than the opposite law of equal partibility, which, in a few generations, would break down the aristocracy of the country, and, by the endless subdivision of the soil, must ultimately be unfavourable to agriculture and injurious to the best interests of the State." These dismal forebodings of the fatal results of a small alteration in the law, which is quite as often resisted on the ground that it would have scarcely any results at all, appear to be founded on a transparent fallacy. If the alternative lay, as the Commissioners seem to have thought, between the law as it now stands, accompanied by the full liberty of bequest we at present enjoy, and a system of *compulsory* equality, with the right of willing either greatly curtailed or completely abolished, we should thoroughly agree with the Commissioners on the pernicious character of such an innovation. But, since it is difficult to believe that the assimilation of the law of realty in its devolution on intestacy to that of personalty would in the course of "a few generations" either "break down the aristocracy of the country" or produce an "endless subdivision of the soil," and since on the other hand we have ample evidence that the present condition of the law does frequently cause very great hardship and distress among the class of small proprietors, there seems to be at least a strong *primâ facie* ground for modifying its provisions.

"Intestacy," says Mr. Joshua Williams, "rarely happens to the owner of large landed property. The property which decends to heirs under intestacies, *though large in the aggregate, is generally small in individual cases.*"* It is precisely in this circumstance that the hardship consists. In the great majority of cases a large estate is resettled, on

* Personal Property, p. 402.

the tenant in tail in remainder attaining his majority or contemplating marriage. After such a settlement, it often happens that little realty remains in the power of either the old or the new life-tenant for him to bequeath by will. Mr. Brodrick agrees that the effects of the law of intestacy on large estates are not extensive; he is however of opinion that cases of voluntary intestacy on the part of large proprietors are especially rare, and that when intestate death occurs it is more often the result of a failure to execute an intention deliberately formed but constantly postponed, or of a will or several wills having been made which the courts are unable to recognise as valid, or perhaps of the recent purchase of some piece of freehold which by the sudden demise of the purchaser devolves upon the heir.* Yet it is an equally admissible view that intestacy among the landowning class, when it does happen, arises from the circumstance that the intestate, having, as he considers, already made by deed suitable provision for all who are interested in his estate, or have a claim on his remembrance, is content that the remainder should devolve upon the heir by course of law, and without the expensive employment of further legal instruments.

It may at least be assumed that among the holders of large estates undesigned intestacy, extending in its effects to any considerable portion of their property, is of comparatively rare occurrence, and that when it occurs it must ordinarily be ascribed to discreditable neglect. The succession of the heir of a large proprietor is usually a very different thing from the nearly "universal succession" of the heir of an intestate owner of a small unsettled freehold. "The settlements," says Mr. Williams, "by which entails are created are more frequently made by deed than by will. They almost invariably contain provisions for the portions of younger children, varying in amount with the value of the property; and whether made by deed or will, they are usually long and intricate in their nature, providing for the numerous contingencies which may arise under the peculiar circumstances

* Cobden Club Essays, p. 68.

of each family. Nothing in fact can be more different than the devolution of an estate to the eldest son under a family settlement, and the descent on an intestacy to the eldest son as heir-at-law. In the one case he takes subject to the proper claims of the other members of his family; in the other he is bound to them by no obligation at all. There seems to be no method of making, in case of intestacy, any sort of disposition of landed property which might be reasonably simple, and at the same time resemble an ordinary family settlement."* Such being the case, the question presents itself, does the existing rule of law, by which the heir takes everything and the next of kin nothing at all, on the whole coincide with the real wishes and intentions of the owners of small freehold estates, or is it the case that, with the great majority of such persons, the failure to make a will arises either from accident or inadvertence or from an impression that the law if left to itself will distribute the property in a very different manner? The prevailing theory is that the law of intestacy has for its object to carry out, as far as can be ascertained, the probable intentions of the deceased himself; and this seems to be, on the whole, the best theory on which such a law can at the present day be based. The results however scarcely seem to be in practical agreement with such a theory. Experience seems to shew that the owner of a small freehold, when he makes his will, usually devises it to trustees for sale, and directs the proceeds to be apportioned among his children in such shares as, regard being had to the provision he has already made for them, the position they may occupy in the world, perhaps too the place they may have acquired in his affections by their respective merits, he on the whole considers best. He does not exclude a daughter for the sake of her brother, or leave the younger children in penury for the questionable object of "making" an eldest son. He has probably acquired the property himself; he has never thought it worth while to settle it; he has failed, possibly through no fault of his own, to execute

---

* Williams, *Personal Property*, pp. 401, 402.

a valid will; he relies, it may be, on the equity of the law; and on his death bed is happily ignorant that his unfortunate relatives will soon discover how little law and equity are as yet in such matters "fused."

One of the principal objections which may be justly urged against the present law lies in the practical difficulty which the layman now constantly experiences—a difficulty which his ancestors but rarely felt—in distinguishing real from personal estate. An advowson, for instance, is at present a marketable commodity, and capable of being bequeathed or descending on intestacy; and yet there are probably many owners of advowsons who are not quite certain whether such property is real or personal, and comparatively few who could explain why it is classed under the former head. There are other cases in which the distinction between realty and personalty depends on reasons still more purely artificial. Thus, shares in railways and canals are ordinarily personal property; but the owner of shares in the New River Company enjoys a freehold estate. A lease of lands for however long a period—a building lease, for instance, for 999 years—is merely a personal interest in the soil; while he who possesses an acre of ground during another's lifetime, in the legal phrase, "hath a freehold." It is thus quite possible to imagine a person owning a large amount of real property dying under the impression that his property was exclusively personal, or *vice versa*. Let us for example take the hypothetical case of two men of business, in the same position of life, and each with a large family which depends upon him for support. Each, having realised a moderate fortune, retires from trade, realises his interest in the firm, and looks out for a suitable investment. One applies his whole capital to the purchase of New River Shares, while the other invests in leasehold property and buys a long and valuable "term of years." They both die intestate, each in the belief that his property is personal and will be divided in due proportion between his widow and children. The intentions of one of them will be exactly realised; while every penny belonging to the other will go to the heir at law, on whose sense of honour and acquaintance with the wishes of the deceased their more or less complete fulfilment will depend. Perhaps, on the other hand, while the owner of the shares deemed his possessions personal, the owner of the leaseholds thought his estate was real; in which case the intentions of each would be alike frustrated. It may of course be replied that such misapprehensions imply an amount of carelessness difficult to conceive and which deserves to be punished; but unfortunately the history of litigation shews that there is scarcely any degree of carelessness, in dealing with property, which can be pronounced incredible; and the law of intestacy is meant to remedy the unfortunate effects of carelessness as well as of accidents which could not be foreseen. And indeed the argument that the forfeiture of posthumous control over property is only a fit punishment for wilful ignorance or neglect seems to lose nearly all its force when we remember that it is not the deceased but his innocent kindred who suffer from the consequences of such errors.

The case above depicted is of course imaginary; but it is not necessary to travel out of the region of actual facts to discover illustrations of the perverse effects too often produced among the poorer class of freeholders by the present law of intestate succession. Many hard cases have been mentioned, during the discussions of the subject in the House of Commons, by Mr. Locke King and others, far too many indeed to be cited here. The writer of an article in *The Times*, who, on the rejection of Mr. Potter's Bill last year, asked why the promoters of that measure failed to adduce instances of substantial wrong inflicted by the law of Primogeniture,[*] had only to look through some former volumes of Hansard to find plenty of such instances recorded in its columns. Hardships, for example, frequently arise from a poor freeholder dying intestate, leaving an infant heir; letters of administration of course cannot be taken out in the same way as if he had left a few hundred pounds in the bank; and the only way to obtain beneficial control

[*] *The Times*, June 29th, 1876.

over the property is by the expensive process of applying to the Chancery Division for the appointment of a trustee.* Another case which actually occurred is that of a parent who by his will bequeathed his property, which was exclusively personal, to his children in equal shares. He afterwards contracted to buy a small freehold estate, but died before the purchase money had been handed over. The executors were of course compelled to complete the purchase. They had to employ nearly all the personalty for that purpose, and the freehold estate went exclusively to the eldest son, who was perhaps an infant. One other instance of the operation of the law given in an earlier debate by Mr. Locke King is so striking that I venture to reproduce his words :—

"A man married a woman who had some property of her own. The House would recollect that among the humbler classes scarcely any settlements were made; and no settlement was made in this case. The man was in trade; but not liking to employ his wife's fortune in his business, it remained untouched for some years. At length the house in which they resided was advertised for sale, and the man at once said to his wife, 'This is a fair investment for your money,' and he bought the house with that money. Some time afterwards the man died, and, not being acquainted with the law, he died intestate. He was extremely fond of his wife, and had no children. What was the result? A nephew of his, the heir-at-law, claimed the property, and the unfortunate widow was obliged to find employment as a menial servant." †

No doubt this case was one of peculiar hardship; but there is no reason to believe that it is at all exceptional in its general features. Hundreds of others have been brought to the knowledge of those who advocate a change in the law, and many of them have been mentioned and not disputed in the House of Commons. On the other hand, if the law of intestate succession to realty were assimilated to that which the Statutes of Distribution have established in the case of personalty, while none who desired to leave their property to the person who, under the present system, is heir-at-law would be prevented from doing so, the occurrence of cases in which not only the known intentions of the

---

* *Hansard's Parliamentary Debates*, cxcvii., 186.
† *Hansard*, clxxxiii., 1976, 7.

deceased are defeated but grievous wrong is inflicted on others would become impossible. No one would have a right to complain; for the person who is now the heir would cease to be so, and would have no pretext for bewailing the disappointment of his legitimate expectations; and if a certain amount of landed property were yearly distributed among the next of kin, instead of going to a single representative, of deceased intestates, it would be impossible to seriously maintain either that the custom of Primogeniture was endangered or the rights of property assailed. It may indeed be contended with some plausibility that the present rule, if its existence, and its consequences as realised in practice, were generally known among the members of the class which it principally affects, would be enough to inspire a positive horror of intestacy, which can scarcely be a desirable feeling in any community. Such horror has been experienced in other lands and times, and it seems to have been engendered by circumstances strikingly analogous to those above referred to. At Rome, as in other ancient States, testamentary disposition was at first unknown. The intestate succession of the family of the deceased to all he owned was there as elsewhere the older rule. The right of willing was at Rome but gradually and tentatively introduced; but at no long period after it was fully established it was very generally exercised, and before the close of the republican period there was no calamity which the Roman citizen regarded as more serious than that of intestate death. The wish that he might die without a will was almost the worst imprecation which a Roman could employ against his most bitter enemy. The reasons which probably actuated this "vehement distaste for an intestacy" are well explained by Sir Henry Maine. "We might have assumed *à priori*," he remarks, "that the passion for testacy was generated by some moral injustice entailed by the rules of Intestate Succession;"* and he proceeds to shew what that moral injustice was. The emancipated children—those in all probability whom the father most loved and honoured—

* *Ancient Law*, p. 222.

suited to the requirements and sentiments of our population, will hesitate, will "think thrice" and perhaps more than thrice, before they assent to any proposal, such as that for the abolition of the liberty of entailing, or the prescription of some plan for the compulsory distribution of landed property, which will by its operation destroy the custom of Primogeniture. Those too who believe that the march of democracy in England is in other directions already far too rapid, and that there is in these days a great and increasing danger of the destruction, through a fanatical pursuit of a chimerical equality, of all true liberty and all that is valuable in individual freedom, will probably deem it their duty to oppose with all their power a subversion of the land-laws which has for its ostentatiously proclaimed object the advancement of the democratic principle. Those lastly who hold, and not without reason, that the existence of a cultivated class of hereditary landowners, of gentle blood, is one of the best securities for culture, and the main obstacle which at present exists to the unquestioned supremacy of a vulgar plutocracy, and the consequent establishment of a condition of life and tone of social opinion in which wealth, no matter how acquired, is considered the one thing needful—a contingency scarcely less disastrous and even more immediately dangerous than the complete triumph of the ochlocratic* theory—will think no exertions too great to maintain an order which, on the whole, regards manners as better than money, and cultured refinement as a more precious possession than sordid and dubious wealth.

It has not seemed necessary in this essay to advert to schemes for the confiscation of the "unearned increment" of land, or the assumption by the State of the active rights of ownership of the soil. I trust I have been justified in regarding such suggestions as outside the region of practical politics. I have confined myself to the examination, necessarily brief and imperfect, of proposals which are advocated every day, and which a sudden revulsion of public feeling

* I venture to avail myself of the word which Polybius (6, 4, 6) employs to denote the worst and basest type of democratic government.

met Mr. Disraeli had succeeded Mr. Gladstone as First Lord of the Treasury. Mr. King himself was not among the members of the new House; and the measure which he had so perseveringly advocated, like many other measures of importance, in favour of which there is no general agitation, has not been included in the legislative programme of the present Government. It was however revived last year; a Bill, similar to those identified with the name of Mr. Locke King, was introduced by Mr. Potter; and it came on for second reading on the 28th of June. The Attorney-General made a rather weak speech against the motion; and it was rejected in a House of nearly four hundred Members by the somewhat small majority of thirty-five.

The view which I have endeavoured to support in the present section may be summed up in very few words. While the Custom of Primogeniture on the whole is beneficial, the Law of Primogeniture is on the whole pernicious. In very many cases it fails to carry out the wishes of those whose intentions it professes to interpret; and it by no means rarely happens that it works grievous wrong to a very deserving class. So far from the retention of all that it is good in the Custom depending on the maintenance of the Law, which is the reverse of good, the cause of the former is really weakened by its liability to be carelessly identified or wilfully confused with that of the latter; and while the assimilation of the law of realty to that of personalty in all cases is a measure of which the expediency is open to question, their assimilation, in the event of intestacy, is a reform of which the principle has been affirmed by the House of Commons, and which we have a right to expect from any future Liberal Administration which deserves the name.

many years ago a childless testator was expected to leave the bulk of his property to his next of kin; but no such "claim of consanguinity" appears at present to be recognised as binding. A time perhaps may come when the obligations of parents in this respect to their own offspring will, under some circumstances, be held to be less stringent than they are now considered.* It may even happen that in process of time, as new feelings spring up and old sentiments lose their force, the Custom of Primogeniture may gradually cease to be a custom. In all these cases there seems to be the strongest *prima facie* reason for leaving the general moral tone to assert itself without legal aid or hindrance; and this argument acquires additional strength, from the point of view of the economist, when we take into consideration the undoubted fact that a free liberty of testamentary bequest, within reasonable limits, forms one of the most powerful incentives to prudence and thrift, to industry and enterprise, in short to all those qualities which tend to the accumulation of wealth and the prosperity of a State.

"With respect to progressive societies," writes Sir Henry Maine,† "it may be laid down that social necessities and social opinion are always more or less in advance of Law.

* "Or again we may take an instance where the alteration is *perhaps actually going on*—the claims of kindred in respect of bequest. We should now commonly think that a man ought to leave his property to his children, unless they had shewn themselves undeserving; but if he has no children we think he may do what he likes with it, unless any of his brothers or sisters are in poverty, in which case compassion seems to blend with and invigorate the evanescent claim of consanguinity. But in an age not long past a childless man was held to be morally bound to leave his money to his collateral relatives; and thus we are naturally led to conjecture that, *in the not distant future,* any similar obligation to children—unless in want—will have vanished out of men's minds." First edition, p. 218: cf. p. 221. A further illustration of Mr. Sidgwick's views may be found in the circumstance that in America, at the present day, a man of great wealth—like the late Mr. Stewart, for instance—is expected by strong public feeling to devote a considerable portion of his fortune, either during his life or by his will, to public or charitable objects; no such feeling however at present exists among ourselves; though Lord Derby, in a recent speech, seemed to imply that wealthy individuals might not unreasonably be asked to contribute more directly to the revenues of the heavily indebted state which protects their wealth.

† *Ancient Law,* p. 24.

We may come indefinitely near to the closing up of the gap between them, but it has a perpetual tendency to reopen. Law is stable; the societies we are speaking of are progressive. The greater or less happiness of a people depends on the degree of promptitude with which the gulf is narrowed."

It may perhaps be doubted whether in a very advanced stage of civilisation, such as that which we now enjoy, this proposition is altogether and uniformly true. It is indeed most advisable that law should follow as closely as possible on the footsteps of morality; but it may be questioned whether in modern society it does not exhibit a tendency not merely to come up with it but to pass it by. "The closing of the gap" is a worthy object of the highest ambition of a genuine statesman; but it is of even greater importance to maintain the respective positions of the two agencies of progress, to leave morality in the place of pioneer, and to beware that law does not usurp the character of an officious guide, instead of contenting itself with the sphere and functions of a faithful follower. In these days in which legislation is so active, and so much of the highest intellect of the country is devoted to suggesting and promoting the amelioration of its laws, the practical danger of positive law advancing too rapidly for current morality is one which we cannot afford to overlook; and it is a danger of which the results, if it were suffered to affect our system of land laws, would assuredly be peculiarly calamitous.

It only remains to state that the conclusions expressed in this essay are the result of a perfectly unbiassed consideration of its subject. The attention which the writer, before the establishment of the Yorke Prize, had devoted to the subject of Primogeniture was chiefly directed to its historical evolution; and this circumstance must be considered mainly responsible for the discussion at the beginning of the essay of the origin of that institution at a length which perhaps requires apology. The writer, on approaching the examination of its effects on the tenure of landed property, was fully prepared to find them so unsatisfactory as to furnish a valid argument for its abolition; but he has been unable to arrive at such a result; and accordingly has not hesitated to express the conclusions to which he has irresistibly been led. It well may be that the views here urged are not altogether such as would have commended themselves to the judgment of the munificent founder of the prize; on this subject the writer has no positive information; but there is one point as to which he feels entire confidence. Mr. Yorke doubtless hoped, when he determined to stimulate by his liberality the study of the law of real property, and especially of the laws of succession, in the University of Cambridge, that those who were attracted to that study by his generous bequest would not hesitate to give expression to their own deliberate opinions; and that if they felt constrained to disagree with what may perhaps have been his own feelings and ideas they would borrow and adapt the well-known phrase of a great essayist of old—*amicus ille, sed magis amica veritas.*

INDEX.

AGR

AGRARIAN laws of Rome, their object, 75.
Agricultural improvements, effected by feudalism, 42. Agricultural system of ancient Italy, causes of its ruin, 75. Agricultural Holdings Act, the, 107-109.
Aids, feudal, their connection with Primogeniture, 37, 38.
Alienation of land, early restrictions on, in England, 12. Permitted before the Conquest, 31. By feudal tenant, at first checked by arbitrary fines, 39. By King's tenants *in capite*, 39. Reasons of objection to it by feudal lord, 40, 41. Efforts to re-establish right of alienating after the Conquest, 43. Permitted *inter vivos* by *Quia emptores*, 45-47. Most complete power of alienating existed under the Tudor and Stuart monarchies, 60. Unfavourably regarded by Greek legislators, 74.
Allod, descent of the German, 11.
American Union, limitation of entails in, 102. Comparative independence of children in, 118.
Aristotle, his account of Greek agrarian legislation, 72-74.
Assimilation, proposed, of law of realty to that of personalty, 111. Ditto, in case of intestate succession, 136, *seqq*. View of Real Property Commissioners on this point, 137. Indirect effects of such assimilation, 144, 145.
Athenian law of succession, 9. Qualified Primogeniture at Athens, 20.
Attornment, at first could not be compelled; now unnecessary, 39.

COM

Austin, Mr. John, on compulsory partition of estates, 92, 93. Approves of large holdings, 93. *See* French.
Austria, proportion of agricultural to total population, and productiveness of soil, 83. Succession law of, 99. Entails occasionally permitted, 99.

BAVARIA, a customary system of Primogeniture preserves holdings of peasant proprietors in, 98, 99.
Belgium, proportion of agricultural to total population, and productiveness of soil, 83. Excessive subdivision of land in, 99, 100.
Benefices, origin of modern Primogeniture among the Beneficiaries, 21, 22. Their history compared with that of the Zemindaries, 22. Their historical relation to feuds, 28, 29.
Blackstone's description of the effects of strict entails, 55, 56.
Bocland, 12. Distinguished from alienable acquisitions, 47.
Bremen, law of intestacy at, 146.
Bright, Mr., his speech at Rochdale, 81.

CELIBACY, reasons for its prohibition in ancient society, 16, 17.
Charters, the Anglo-Saxon, 32.
Code Napoleon, the, restored substitutions within narrow limits, 53. Its rules subversive of large estates, 75. Established perpetual entails, 88, 89.
Collusive recoveries of entailed estates, 57, 58.
Companions of the King, their status, 28.

CON

Consanguinity, ancient society, based on, 14.
Contingent remainders, 61, 62.
Continuity of the ancient family, 17.
Cornwallis, Lord, his permanent settlements, 7.
Corvées, the, 87.
Coulanges, M. F. de., on the ancient family, 15. His view of the effects of religious feeling, 15, 16.

DEMOCRACY, and plutocracy, dangers of their progress in England, 152.
De Tocqueville, M., on subdivision of French estates, 89. On the effects of democracy on paternal power, 118. His explanation of democratic form of civil legislation of modern France, 119. Remarks on the evil of a wealthy aristocracy without political privileges, 129. On the influence of succession laws on Society, 150.
Domesday Book, causes which led to its compilation, 33, 34. The New, 78.

ECONOMICAL utility of Primogeniture in early times, 41, 42.
Eldest son, his religious duties as representative of the family in India, Greece, and Rome, 19. His representative and political privileges in India, Germany, Scotland, and Ireland, 20. Substituted in deeds for 'heir,' 61. His position in a settled estate, 63.
Emphyteusis, origin and development of system of, 26, 27.
England and France, their comparative productiveness of soil, 82, 83.
Entails, not unknown at Rome, 51. In England since *De donis*, 53. Their history in Scotland, 63-68. Scotch, their effect on agriculture, 68, 69. System of perpetual entails established by the Code Napoleon, 88, 89. Suggested abolition of, accompanied by full liberty of conveyance and bequest, 101. Said to prejudice landlord's freedom and tenant's security, 104-107.

GAR

Escheat, rule of, indirectly supported Primogeniture, 40.

FACULTY of Advocates, the, opposed perpetual entails, 66.
Family, the ancient, its connection with the land, 14. View of M. de Coulanges, 15, 16. Its continuity, 17. Germ of primogeniture in position of eldest son, 18. Family relations, how affected by custom of Primogeniture, 115, 116. By compulsory partition and by free liberty of bequest, 117.
Fee, its etymology, 29.
Female infanticide, its effects on family life, 3.
Feoffment to purchasers, his heirs and assigns, subsequently furnished a general rule of construction, 48.
Feetail, dates from *De donis*, 49. *See* Entails.
Feuda, individua, 36. *Nova ut antiqua*, 43.
Feudal system of tenure, its characteristics, 24. Its connection with Roman law, 25-27. Introduced into England by the Normans, 27. Its destruction in France at the revolution, 86, 87.
Fines, their close connection with Primogeniture, 39. Their history, 58, 59.
Forfeitures of Scotch estates, 65.
France, *see* England. Subdivision of estates in, 88-91. The population of, almost stationary, 97.
Frank-marriage and frankalmoign, 46, 47.
Frederick Barbarossa, constitution of, 36.
Freeman, Mr., his explanation of the non-existence in England of any class of nobles, 121, 122.
Free trade, feeling against in France, 96.
French succession law, political origin of the modern, 86, 87. Austin's remarks on its probable effects, 92-95.

GARNIER, M., on price of small estates in France, 92.
Gastrell, Mr. Harris, on land-tenure in Prussia, 97, 98.

Gavelkind, Irish, 12. In Kent, 80, n., 144, n.
Greece, ancient, method of regulating land-tenure in, 72-74.
Green, Mr. J. R., on confiscations effected by King William, 34, 35.

Heirs of landowners, effects of rule of Primogeniture on, 116.
Hereditary peerage, the, attacks on its legislative power, 129.
Holland, proportion of its agricultural to total population, and productiveness of soil, 83. Feeling in, opposed to sub-division of estates, 100.

Indian laws of succession, 4. Partition not usual; when it occurred, the land divided into equal lots, 5. Tenure by the Zemindars, 85-7. Indian laws do not recognise wills, 8.
Intestacy, equal distribution on, in India, Greece, Germany, England and Ireland, 13. Devolution of realty and personalty on, 134. Dislike of, among Roman citizens, 143. Succession on, in America and at Bremen, 146.
Irish gavelkind and tanistry, 12.
Italy, proportion of its agricultural to total population, and productiveness of soil, 83.

Joint ownership of land, its effects on agriculture, 41, 42.
Justinian, legislation of, adverse to entails, 52

Keltic Primogeniture, 20.
King, Mr. Locke, his Real Estate Intestacy Bills, 146-148.
Knight's tenure, descent of land under, 35. Personal service attached to, 40. Abolition of Knight's service, 59.

Landed property, its tenure and inheritance before the Conquest, 31. Held of the Crown throughout the Kingdom, 35. Right of the State to determine conditions of its tenure, 70. State regulations concerning, in ancient Greece, 72-74. Comparatively small number of proprietors in England, 76. Vast number in France, 77. Parliamentary Return of English landowners, 78-80.
Leslie, Mr. Cliffe, on French agricultural system, 91.
Local self-government, English system of, depends on custom of Primogeniture, 130, 131.
Lycurgean partition, the alleged, in Sparta, 73.
Lytton, Lord, on Austrian agriculture, 99.

Maine, Sir H., on relation of law to social opinion, 154, 155. See also references, *passim*.
Manu, laws of, recognise a kind of Primogeniture, 20.
Maritagium, right of, recognised by Statute of Merton, 39.
Marriage, restricted in Wurtemburg by communal regulations, 98.
McCulloch, Mr. J. R., believes a system of Primogeniture to have existed at Rome, 10. Remarks on entailed land in Scotland, 67.
McLennan, Mr., on primitive marriage, 3.
Metayer tenantry, their origin, 27. Contemporary prevalence of the system in France, 91.
Military tenures, question whether they were known in England before the Conquest, 30. Military testament, origin of Roman entails in, 51.
Mir, the Russian, its system of cultivation, 42.
Monogamy preceded by polyandry, 3.
Montalembert on entails in England, 114.
Morality, public, its influence on systems of succession, 153.

Neate, Mr., on proportion of land affected by *De donis* and by *Quia emptores* respectively, 54.
Nobility, no order of, exists in England, 121. In France, 123-125. The noble prefix *de* fraudulently assumed, 124.

Ordonnance d'Orleans, limited duration of substitutions, 53.

Oxford and Cambridge, colleges at, founded subsequently to *De donis*, 55.
Oxylus, his scheme for perpetuating ancestral estates, 74.

PARLIAMENTARY Return of owners of land, 78-80. Debates on Intestate Succession to Realty, 146-149.
Peasant proprietors in France, their supposed security, 95, 96.
Peerage, the English, an elastic body, 123. Hereditary, its legislative powers attacked, 129.
Permanent Settlements of Lord Cornwallis, 7.
Perpetual entails in Scotland, 66.
Personalty, law of, proposed assimilation of law of realty to, 111. Origin of the distinction, 112. Distribution of, on intestacy, 135, 136.
Phaleas of Chalcedon, his agrarian law, 73.
Plato objected to disposition of landed property by will, 11. Suggests a limit of inequality in property, 74.
Polyandry, monogamy preceded by, 3.
Population, increase of, a test of national prosperity, 96. Very small increase in recent years in France, 97.
Portugal, effects of excessive subdivision in, 101.
Posthumous life of the eponymous progenitor; influence of belief in, 15, 16.
Prima seisina, 38.
Primitive family life, origin of Primogeniture in, 2.
Proprietary privileges of eldest son, disappear in more advanced stage of social life, 4. Growth of the Chief's proprietary rights, 21.
Protection, demanded by French industry and agriculture, 96.
Prussia, proportion of agricultural to total population, and productiveness of soil in, 83. Its agricultural system, 97.

REALTY and personalty, distinction between, occasionally merely technical, 140.

Recoveries, collusive, 57, 58.
Register, public, of entails in Scotland, 64.
Reliefs, their effect on inheritance of eldest son, 38.
Roman agrarian legislation, its object, 75.
Russian Mir, the, its system of cultivation, 42. Proportion of agricultural to total population, and productiveness of soil, 83.
Russian nobility, the, 125-127. Only distinction in Russia that of official rank, 126.

SACRA, the, at Rome and in India, 18.
Scotch entails, their history, 63-68. First introduced in 1648, 64. Scotch tenant in tail, his present position, 68.
Scutage or escuage, commutation of personal service for, 43.
Semitic custom of primogeniture, 1.
Services annexed to tenure, and services annexed to land, 33.
Settlement, a modern, its nature and effects, 63. Of personalty, 112, 113.
Shelley's case, 60.
Sidgwick, Mr. H., on pecuniary obligations to kindred, as determined by common sense morality, 153, 154.
Smith, Adam, on Scotch entails, 67.
Socage, descent of socage lands, 35, 36.
Social value of a class of hereditary landowners, 131, 132.
Society, ancient, based on consanguinity, 14.
Spain, proportion of agricultural to total population, and productiveness of soil in, 83. Large extent of soil still subject to entail in, 101.
Spartan system of land tenure, 72, 73.
Stubbs, Professor, on relation of military service to tenure before the Conquest, 32, 33.
Subdivision of soil, evils of excessive, 84, 85.
Subinfeudation, at first an integral part of the feudal system; not permitted to tenants *in capite*, 44. Abolished by Quia emptores, 45.

Its effects on the heir's prospects. 46.
Substitutions, vulgar and pupillar, were not entails, 51. In France, 52, 53.
Succession laws, in India, 4, 5. At Athens, Sparta and Rome, 9-11. In France, political origin of the modern, 86, 87. The French, widely imitated by other European States, 88. De Tocqueville on their importance, 150.

TALTARUM'S case, 57.
Tanistry in Ireland, 12.
Ten thousand acres, number of owners of, in England, 81.
Tenants *in capite*, 35. Alienation by, 39, 40. Subinfeudation by, not permitted, 44.
Tenure of landed property, its conditions, a matter of public policy, 151.
Testamentary power, introduced by English courts in Lower Bengal, 8. Ancient restrictions on its exercise, in India and at Athens, 11. Plato's objection to its exercise, 11. Plenary, supposed to have been conceded by the XII. tables, 13, 14. Exercised in England before the Conquest, 31. Restored by Statute of Wills, 59. Originally unknown at Rome, 143.
Transfer of land, attempts to facilitate; need of a general system of registration and simplification of forms, 109, 110.

Trinoda necessitas, the, 32.
Trusts, express and tacit, 52.

USES, doctrine of, first developed in the time of Edward III., 55.

VICTORIA, aspect of the land-tax question in, 71.

WARDSHIP, its theory and limits, 38.
West, Mr. Sackville, on subdivision of estates in France, 90.
William the Conqueror, extensive redistribution of land effected by, 34.
Wills, *see* Testamentary Power.
Wurtemburg, succession law of, 98. Qualified custom of primogeniture in small holdings, 98. Marriage restricted by communal regulations, 98.
Wyndham, Mr., on partition of small holdings in Belgium, 100.

YORKE, Mr. C., on forfeitures for treason, 65.
Younger sons, how affected by Primogeniture; advantages enjoyed by the cadet of an ancient family, 119-121.

ZEMINDARS and Talookdars, their origin and position, 5, 6. History of their power, 6. Primogeniture among the Zemindars unfavourably regarded by British administrators, 6, 7.